R

FAE PRINCE

BESTSELLING AUTHOR
Natasha Luxe

Published by Rare Books 2022
http://thepennandluxe.com/
Copyright © 2022 Natasha Luxe

ALSO BY NATASHA LUXE

Celebrity Crush Series

MEET CUTE
PLOT TWIST
OFF CAMERA

The *Heroes and Villains* Series with Liza Penn:
Bring your superhero fantasies to life…

NEMESIS
ALTER EGO
SECRET SANCTUM
MAGICIAN
THUNDER
GODDESS

Never miss a sexy release! Join my mailing list:

https://rarebooks.substack.com/welcome

CHAPTER 1: SLOANE

I know it's a dream, but I don't care.

The haze that wraps around me is that perfect fog of not dead-asleep but not fully awake, when my body is all tingly relaxed and my brain is free to roam and play. And they always say your brain can't tell the difference between made-up fantasies and reality, right? So I lie in bed, willing my mind to stay in this moment, and dream.

The dream is always the same—at least, when I can choose it like this.

I'm standing in the towering central hall of Fort Precipice. The midnight black stone of the walls, floor, and ceiling swirls at the farthest reaches of my vision, broken by pinprick flickers of the softest yellow candlelight. That singular description has been the basis of a long-running comparison in the fandom: that standing in Fort Precipice's central hall is like floating weightless in the starry night sky. So for a moment, I'm just a star floating among the stars.

And oh, I *am* a star, at least in this dress. A gown of gilded silver and gold tucks snug against my breasts and follows the rise and dips of my body to trail behind the equally daring pointed heels on my feet. I'm all glitter and sin as I take one step, then another, slowly following the embroidered runner from the back of the room all the way to the waiting dais at the front.

All the way to Kilian.

He's perched on the edge of his throne, one hand gripping the armrest like he's either holding himself back or preparing to shove himself forward. His shoulders cave, heaving on tight breaths that match the intense scowl on his handsome face.

He is not pleased to see me.

"You dare come here," he starts, a bellow that ricochets through his hall, "alone and unarmed. Did you think you would be welcomed?"

I stop at the edge of the dais. My heart flutters, tickling all the way up my throat, and I swallow, peeking at him through the curling tendrils of my hair.

"It is not welcome I have come for," I say, and *oh*, the thrill of that line. How many times have I read it? But still thinking it sends a sharp, delicious shiver between my legs.

God, I'm already aching, my whole body heating up so I know my chest is flushed. Does he notice?

He does.

Of course he does.

Kilian Kilnmor, high prince of Fort

Precipice, the most powerful fae in the realm, would be able to hear the speed of my pulse. He'd be able to smell the scent of me, excitement dampening my panties. He'd know exactly what is behind my intention, just as he knew his enemy queen's intentions in the book.

He rises from his throne, his body flexing and reforming methodically so I can spot each muscle through the tight black fabric of his clothes. He's lean but strong, muscular yet thin, every inch of him intentional, sculpted, perfected. All of that reflects most strongly in his face, the sharp edges of his unforgiving jaw framing a face inspired by marble-worshipped Greek gods.

Behind him, snapping out wide, his obsidian wings fill the hall from side to side before folding back in. A reminder of who he is, as if I could forget. A threat of what he can do to me.

Kilian takes a single step down the dais. "You bypassed my guards to be here."

I run my tongue across my lips, wetting them. "I did."

He takes another step.

An instinctual pull to retreat tears at me, but I hold strong, somehow keeping my eyes on his. This close, I can see the light in them. Blue eyes rimmed with violet, the sole source of brightness in a world of night. His eyes are the stars; the rest of him is the swath of infinity that has crushed souls far more resilient than I am.

He stops one step above me. His towering size has him dominating the space even more. I don't miss the way his eyes dip to my cleavage—he lingers there, wanting me to see him appraising me, before he looks back up.

And smiles.

It's a cutting smile. A cruel smile. A smile that came from having to claim his position too young and fight his entire life in wars to keep it. And while there is fury in that smile, there is also pain; and it is that pain that has me lifting my hand, reaching to cup his jaw.

He allows it.

For a moment.

Then he seizes my wrist.

His grip is tight, barely painful, a subtle reminder like everything else about him.

The look in his eyes turns feral, his pupils dilating. "You will regret coming to me, Isaura," he purrs.

The name from his lips sends a shock through me.

Isaura. The character in the book. I've played out this scenario so many times, always as her—so why does it gnaw at me this time? Why do I wish I could twist this scene, have him say my name—*Sloane*?

Maybe I can. Maybe I can go back. Have

him say my name—

In my bed, I wriggle deeper into my blankets. Fuck. *Fuck*. No—it's starting to slip—

"I regret a great many things in my life," I say to Kilian. *Isaura* says to Kilian. "But I do not foresee myself capable of regretting you."

Not Isaura. *Me.*

The lines are fading—I can feel sunlight on my face, can smell my automatic coffee maker brewing—

Fuckity fuck *fuuuuck*—

Kilian uses his grip on my wrist to drag me with him as he walks backwards to his throne.

On my bed, I'm slipping my hand down my body, past the elastic on my underwear, fingers diving right into my folds. The fog of fantasy is too thin already, but I'm so hot and tense, my body wound and aching—I *need* it.

I need *him*.

In the book, they fuck on his throne.

He doesn't even take off his clothes, but he makes Isaura undress, and she rides him with his wings spread. He uses his fingers to make her come while she's on him, his impressive cock wet with her juices as she heaves her body up and down, and she bites her lips to silence her cries of pleasure. But when he makes her stand on the armrests of the throne, her pussy even with his face, he eats her out so expertly that her screams draw in his guards.

He lets them watch.

So does she.

It's one of the hottest, most descriptive sex scenes in the series, so fantastically dirty that the bulk of fanart for it is basically just porn. So getting off to it in this little fantasy won't be hard—

The alarm on my phone trills.

And with that, the dream-fantasy fades completely.

I fling my covers back, dig the heels of my palms into my eyes, and whimper.

Fuck.

It's one thing to be left sexually frustrated. Can't say it hasn't happened before.

It's another to be left with this…hole in my chest.

"Isaura," I imagine Kilian saying. A bolt of jealousy spears through me.

The hole aches more.

Am I that lonely that I'm legitimately pining for a fictional guy?

But fuck, why even deny it.

Yes, I am that lonely, because all the real life guys I manage to date are just so…so…*tasteless* compared to Kilian. He's absolutely ruined me for anything real.

I mean, would a real guy singlehandedly fight through an enemy's *entire battalion* because his fear for my life drove him to godlike strength?

Would a real guy spend months wooing me, finding out all of my richest desires, and then commit himself to making them come true, even at the expense of his own needs?

Would a real guy lock me in a dungeon to protect me from enemy forces—well, okay, that definitely wouldn't be as sexy IRL as it is in the book, but still.

I drop my head to the right to see the stack of books on my bedside table. The one I'd been reading last night is on top—*Fort of Night and Edge*. The second book in the *Night Prince and Dawn Queen* series, the one with the aforementioned insanely spicy sex scene.

I've read it seven times now. I've read just that spicy scene—well, let's not put an exact number on it.

Maybe it is getting unhealthy, this obsession.

Maybe it is detrimental to my actual functioning life.

My phone beeps again, my alarm angry that I haven't turned it off. Somewhere beyond my window, a garbage truck whirls as it gets to work; the city is waking up, and so am I.

I scrub my eyes again, my body still aching and unsatisfied, but there's a weird layer of sadness over everything now.

Reality awaits.

And it can really just go fuck itself.

Jacked Up is dead.

I don't mind—especially after this morning's disappointing start. But it always puts my boss in a pissy mood, so I do my best to look busy, wiping down unused café tables and refilling the espresso grinder and doing inventory on the bundled stacks of to-go cups. Kyle stays at the register, going over receipts, grumbling as he glances at the door and back again.

"Fucking chain shops," he says to himself, but I know he wants a response. Especially when he says it again. Slightly louder. "Fucking chain shops."

I don't pause where I'm sweeping the floor between two of the high tops. "Yeah. The worst."

Eden's supposed to get in for her shift in thirty. If I can just hold out until then, I won't be the sole receiver of our boss's monologues. Most men *of a certain age* have perfected the ability to have one sided conversations. Kyle hasn't so much perfected it as he just does it at louder decibels.

Kyle scratches his jowls. "That new complex is gonna run us to the ground. They're opening more new shit. Some club now. And a spa place. And a big gaudy chain restaurant—what's the one—Cheesecake—"

I whip an excited look at him. "Really? Oh my god, I love that place!"

The words die under the withering stare he gives me.

Okay, see, this is why real life men just *suck*. I feel that suck down to the tip of my toes as I stand there, an employee half this asshole's age, knowing that the only reaction I have in my arsenal is to just apologize for disagreeing with him and go back to being silent so he can talk at me until Eden gets here and tips the scale in favor of my gender.

And where usually I do that, now, it just pisses me *off*.

Because Kilian would fucking *murder this guy*.

In fact, the image of Kilian, wings splayed, a glistening sword in his hand, towering over Kyle the Mid-Life Crisis Manager of Jacked Up Coffee House, makes a demonic smile crawl across my face.

Unfortunately, Kyle is still staring at me.

"You got a problem?" he snaps at my grin.

Fuck this guy.

Before I can say something to likely get me fired—now is *not* the time, Sloane, god—the doorbell chimes.

I whip toward the customer, on grateful autopilot. "Hi, welcome to Jacked Up. What can I get you?"

The woman smiles at me. In a sleek scarlet dress and trim overcoat, she's completely put together, the kind of polished business persona that wreaks of hedge funds.

So when she doesn't immediately order a triple shot espresso, my eyebrows go up.

She holds out a stack of fliers. "I own the club that recently opened down the street. I was hoping you could set out these fliers for your customers?"

I take the stack just as Kyle thunders around the counter.

"Absolutely not." He snatches the stack from my hands and I freeze, eyes darting between my idiot boss and the businesswoman.

Her expertly manicured brow lifts. "And why not?"

"That damn complex is killing my business! You can take your fliers and shove them up your ass. We don't support what's going on."

My cheeks flush. Usually Kyle only acts this belligerent around employees he pays to torture— but to say all this shit around someone else?

I start to get out a stammered apology when the woman shoots me a look I understand in one flash.

Don't make it hard on yourself. I got this.

I swallow and stay quiet.

She turns back to Kyle and her eyes dip

once to his name tag. "Ah. Kyle. There seems to be a misunderstanding. You are upset about the chain coffee shop that opened?"

"Damn right."

"Angry that big corporations are squashing the little people?"

Kyle puffs out his chest. "Hell yeah. I—"

"Is Jacked Up not also a chain? Or am I mistaken?" Her tone says *I am never fucking mistaken.*

My eyes widen and I fight hard not to sputter a laugh.

Kyle's mouth shuts. "Well yeah. But—"

"Since you are on the side of the *little people* even though you yourself are part of the *big corporations*, it would be a fantastic show of that support to put these fliers on your counter, given that I am the sole owner of my club. I suspect you are the owner of this establishment?" The woman rests her hand on the stack of fliers in Kyle's hands. Her smile is all sweetness and gratitude. "I greatly appreciate your support, business owner to business owner."

She played him. Hard. And I start to think *there's no fucking way he doesn't see it*—

When Kyle beams. Something shifts in his eyes—offense to pride. "I'd be glad to. Us business owners gotta stick together."

"Indeed." The woman's smile holds.

Kyle shoves the fliers back into my hands.

"Put these on the counter."

I cut my eyes to the woman, stunned out of my mind. Eden and I will have a good laugh about this later. Has Kyle been this easy to play the whole time? Well, fuck.

I stumble to the counter and arrange the fliers in an orderly stack as the woman takes her leave. Kyle heads toward his office at the back, and when I glance through the wall of glass windows that show the street out front, I see the woman walk up to a man who's leaning against a light pole, waiting for her. He's just as put together as she is, in a sleek suit that hugs each of his lean muscles, and even though the window is kind of warped, he's the single most attractive man I've ever seen in my life. Long dark hair, piercing green eyes—he actually stops me short, a flier in my hands, my jaw open, gaping like a moron.

The guy through the window catches me staring. He nods, face expressionless, and I whirl my back to him just as the woman hooks her arm with his and turns to see what he's looking at.

Good lord. Be ruder, Sloane, really.

The back door chimes, and a second later, Eden comes trudging in. "Did we get the holiday blends in yet? I am *so* craving that gingerbread flavored…what's that?"

She bends over my shoulder to look at the flier I'm still holding.

My eyes drop to it and I actually read it for the first time. Which I probably should've done before Kyle agreed to set them out—what kind of club even is it?

The first line of the flier is in bright, swirling script: *Welcome to Club Reverie, where your dreams become your reality...*

Here, your favorite fictional worlds become real.

Virtual reality is a thing of the past. Club Reverie is the future.

Reality has no limitations.

"What on earth?" Eden laughs. "I gotta clock in. What kind of mood are we dealing with today?"

"Um—" My brain trips.

Your favorite fictional worlds become real.

Eden snaps at me. "Sloane—mood. What am I walking into?"

"I—he's fine. Normal. Just don't talk about the usual stuff."

"So basically anything. Got it." Eden trudges off, daring to enter the backroom that's half Kyle's office, half our break area.

But I'm too stuck on this flier. On this...this *Club Reverie.*

Reality has no limitations.

There's an address across the bottom. It's barely a five minute walk from here.

I fold the flier and stuff it into my back pocket.

CHAPTER 2: SLOANE

I get off work just after the lunch rush—which is, surprisingly, a decent rush, and puts Kyle in a good mood, so the workday ends on a better note than it started. I even have a nice wad of tips that I shove into my bag next to my copy of *Fort of Night and Edge*. As I leave Jacked Up, the autumn air makes me shiver, and I burrow deeper into my oversized hoodie.

     I pause for a minute on the sidewalk.

     Right takes me back to my apartment.

     Left takes me to the address on the flier that has somehow found its way back into my hands.

     I turn nonchalantly. I don't know why my chest is tight—I'm just checking out this new club. It doesn't even sound like a *club*, more like a gaming center. Virtual reality something. Maybe it's more of a *members* type club, not a *dance* club—ugh, I'm stalling. In my own head. Brilliant.

     As I walk, I slide the flier into my bag and pull out my book. It's half security blanket, half nervous twitch, but I honestly don't care. And I know the address of where I'm going—a straight shot down this road, then a right turn at the next intersection. And it's midday, so the sidewalk traffic is minimal.

I crack open the book to read as I walk. Dangerous? Maybe. The threat of tripping and face-planting is high. But the moment my eyes crest over the pages, a sense of release settles in me.

Fuck, I am in trouble.

I'd rather be here, doing this, than living my actual life.

Before I can berate myself about how absolutely pathetic that is, I start reading one of my favorite comfort scenes: right before the final climax—the *plot* climax, not a *climax climax*. Well, it is right before Kilian and Isaura fuck for the last time in this book, only Isaura knows that she won't be able to come back. So to her, it truly is the last time.

"I cannot let you walk out of this fort," Kilian says. His voice is flushed, a deep rumble that only serves to stoke the flames in Isaura's heart.

But even so, she turns to the door, eyeing it as one of ice would shy from flames. The moonlight through the window is the only light, giving Kilian's bedchamber a fogged, dreamlike hue, and as she turns to look once more at him, she knows the sight she strikes: a goddess trimmed in starlight, the exact sort of figure that would most fit in the court of Precipice. She can see it in Kilian's eyes as he looks at her—he will ask her to stay, not because she is his enemy and he cannot be seen to show weakness, but because he loves her.

He loves her.

Isaura feels that through every fiber of her body, through every lingering remnant of his touch upon her skin.

He loves her.

And she loves him.

She was never supposed to love him.

"You will stay, Isaura," he tells her. "You will stay and we will join our lands. Be my queen. Stay at my side."

He says it with all the commanding force of his presence. He is a high prince. He has created a court of earned loyalty and unerring dedication. He is used to being obeyed, even by her.

But only when she chooses it.

Steeling up the last vestiges of her strength—how does she have any left? She has drawn on it too much—she turns to him. And there he is, close enough to touch, close enough that she could melt into his arms and confess the true reason she leaves him when she wants to be nowhere else but here.

She almost says it.

The words almost pass her lips.

If she tells him, he could save her. They could fight the true threat together. He thinks she is his greatest enemy; he thinks this war is simple; she only need open her lips to tell him the truth—

But she cannot.

The binding magic jolts through her, reminding her of the contract she made. Tears prick her eyes, and when she looks up at Kilian, he can see in her face that something is wrong.

But she will not tell him.

Cannot tell him.

She cups his jaw, her palm fitting there like it was made to hold him, and arches up onto the toes of her shoes to link her lips with his. How many times has she kissed these lips, and yet each time it is anew, a spark and sizzle of passion that will be her utmost undoing. This man has enchanted her, enriched her in ways she had long given up on. It is poetic in a way he will never know: he has brought sunlight to her world, the world of the Dawn Queen, while she will be the final dusk of the Night Prince.

Isaura whimpers at the ever-hungry gnawing in her chest. No, she will not be his final night—but she is human still, mortal and weak, and now that her lips are on him, she cannot deny herself one last time.

Kilian hears her whimper, or feels it maybe, the wash of all her sorrow too great to stay trapped in her body alone. He starts to pull back, space between them, but no; there will be no space, no pause, no thought.

Isaura reaches for the straps of her thin gown and lets them trickle down her arms, the whole of the fabric pooling at her feet. She is naked now against him, and his arms immediately encircle her body, holding her flush to him, and the softest groan escapes his throat. That he is as enchanted by her as she is by him only serves to dizzy her more, and she fumbles in growing need at the buttons of his shirt, the latch of his belt.

"Isaura," Kilian moans. His fingers glide around her hips and brush reverently across the soft hair at the apex of her thighs. "On the bed. Spread your legs for me."

"I want you inside of me. Now." She manages not to whimper again, but the tension in her voice is mistaken for desire.

Kilian smiles against her mouth. "You will have me. But only once you are dripping for me, my love. Only once your body is unwound will I push us both to that last glorious edge."

I snap the book shut. Okay, so I haven't perfected the ability to read straight-up smut in public, and I know my cheeks are flaming red.

But I'm here, anyway. Club Reverie stands over me, a nondescript single door under a sign that displays its name in simple curling letters that glow a soft neon purple.

Part of me wants to finish this scene. I need Isaura's strength. She went to Kilian after they'd met the first time intending to assassinate him. She went the second time intending the same, but knowing she could seduce him to make it easier.

But when she went the third time.

The fourth time.

And every time after.

She fell more and more in love with him, and that was never part of the plan—because she'd made a deal with a powerful archmage to have the power to kill her greatest enemy at the cost of her own life. If she doesn't kill Kilian, she will die.

He helps her defeat the archmage and break the spell, of course—and the twist about who the archmage actually is to Kilian still sends me *reeling*—but god, the strength Isaura possessed to fight the curse compelling her to murder the man she'd fallen in love with. To go back to him, again and again, because the sweetness of being with him was more important the pain of being near him.

I laugh at myself. Am I really comparing Isaura's situation to the one I'm in? Because yeah, being nervous about going into some weird VR club is totally the same thing as being doomed to murder the man you love.

Fucking hell, Sloane. Get a grip on yourself.

But I'm really, really afraid all sense of *grip* is long gone.

I hold the book to my chest and push inside Club Reverie.

CHAPTER 3: SLOANE

The inside of Club Reverie matches the sign: seductive simplicity.

A small welcome area is done in rich purples and dark blues. A few sleek leather chairs cluster around a low coffee table and a lush green plant dominates the corner. There's a closed door directly across from me, and just next to it is a tall curved reception counter where a woman about my age sits. She immediately looks up and gives a smile I know too well from my work at Jacked Up.

"Welcome to Club Reverie," she says. "How can I make your dreams come true?"

I blanch. I can't help it.

The woman laughs. "I know, right? But it's policy." She pulls up a chilled bottle of water, condensation beading down the plastic. She slides it towards me across the marble countertop. "Now, how can I help you, Miss—"

"Sloane. And, um—I'm not sure yet." I take the water bottle for lack of something to do with my hands, only I'm still holding *Fort of Night and Edge*, so I'm unable to open the bottle.

The woman's eyes go to my book as I clamp my jaw, locked in supremely stupid awkwardness.

"Ah!" she chirps. "I love that series."

Oh thank god. "Me too! Obviously. This copy's seen better days."

"I know Kilian is the ultimate love interest," she sighs, "but I can't help but be sad that Isaura didn't end up with Ambrose."

My brain short circuits. "*What*? Oh my god! But Ambrose was such an abusive jerk! He was working against her from the start——"

The woman's smiling at me in that kind of *aren't you cute* way.

My mouth snaps shut.

"And here I am, yelling my fan theories at someone whose name I don't even know." I tap the closed water bottle against my forehead. "Okay. Well. I'm just going to go smother myself under all my copies of this series."

I don't even get a chance to turn before someone steps out of the doorway beside the counter. I hadn't heard the door open, but from the darkness emerges the woman who'd dropped off the fliers at Jacked Up.

Her eyes dip up and down my body, a curious look on her face, like she's trying to discern my life story from my faded hoodie, scuffed work shoes, dented messenger bag, and the frizz my hair has become. But she blinks, breaking out of the analysis, and when she smiles at me, I stop my retreat.

There's something in her smile.
Something…promising.

"Actually, Sloane, I think you're in exactly
the right place," she says. "I'm Devyn Namara. I'm
pleased my encounter with your boss this morning
did not set you against my club."

"The exact opposite, honestly. I'm sorry
about what Kyle——"

Devyn waves her hand. "His actions are not
yours to apologize for. We do not take on the
burdens of lesser men."

Well, fuck, can't argue with that.

Devyn steps aside and motions into the
darkness beyond the open door. "I assume you are
interested in what Club Reverie has to offer?"

My eyes dart back to the receptionist. She
gives a reassuring smile, and when she pulls out a
tablet with a padded stylus—ah, paperwork, of
course—Devyn stops her with an *I've got this one*
nod.

"Shall we?" Devyn asks me.

I swallow. Again.

I'm here, aren't I?

"Sure." I step beyond and Devyn shuts the
door behind me.

I have to blink a few times before my eyes catch the
low light. A hall stretches to my left and right, the
walls lined with floor to ceiling sections of glass

that show a dozen rooms. Some are dark; some panes of glass are frosted; but Devyn leads me toward one that's empty, the glass clear, the room within lit by the same soft white light that gives the hall that seductive, cozy feel.

"Have you ever used a VR console before, Sloane?" Devyn asks as she holds the door for me.

I duck inside, shaking my head. On my Jacked Up salary, I'm lucky to fuel my reading habit, let alone gaming. It's the only hobby I can afford.

Devyn ushers me to sit on what looks like a dentist chair, which is a really unfortunate comparison that almost breaks the whole mysterious-sexy vibe of this place, only the moment I do sit, the chair is so soft and decadent that I actually moan.

Devyn grins. "I know, right? I should rebrand this place as strictly for luxury napping."

"You know what, I'd buy into that."

A table near the chair holds a similar tablet to the one that the receptionist had, and Devyn slides it into her hands. "As I was saying—it's good, actually, that you have no previous VR familiarity, because Club Reverie is unlike anything else on the market today. It's a fully realistic sensory experience. Using a specially designed headset—" She points above me, and I jolt to see a futuristic-looking space helmet contraption hidden in the ceiling. "—we're able to safely tap into all of a user's senses. You see, feel, taste, hear, and smell your fantasy as if it were real."

"My…fantasy?" I tear my eyes away from the space helmet to give Devyn a confused frown.

She nods at the book in my lap. "The world of *Night Prince and Dawn Queen* is one you would like to visit?"

I laugh. More like *guffaw*. It breaks out of me so abruptly that Devyn cuts another grin, and I feel my cheeks go lava hot.

"Um. Yeah," I stammer. "Sure. *Of course.* Who wouldn't? But it's not like—"

"That's one of the more popular destinations." Devyn taps on the screen in her hands before swiveling it to me.

There, splayed across the tablet, is an image of Fort Precipice. The screen holds a number of prompts ranging from *Location* to *Scene* to—

"Does that say *Characters*?" I gape up at Devyn.

She pulls the tablet back to tap something across the screen. "You're a fan of Kilian Kilnmor, I heard? Would it be out of line to assume that your ideal fantasy would involve the scene from Chapter 10 of the second book?"

"I—wait, *what*? What are you talking about? Like, I'd play a video game as Isaura or something?"

"Well, that's fair. This isn't *technically* the

world of *Night Prince and Dawn Queen*—but we are working on copyright agreements. For now, it's an almost exact replica. But you would not be playing Isaura. You would be yourself, Sloane, in a very close approximate to the world and plot of *Fort of Night and Edge*. Should you wish to carry the plot of Isaura, you can. Should you wish to take the plot in other directions based on your choices, you can as well. There is no limit to the possibility in Club Reverie. Your fantasy is yours to control."

I think I have tears in my eyes.

Which is just horrifically embarrassing.

"You're saying I could play around in *Fort of Night and Edge*. Or close to it. And it'd feel real?"

There must be too much hope in my voice. Too much *need*.

Because Devyn's expression breaks a little, and she taps to something else on the screen before passing the tablet back to me.

As I suspected earlier—waivers. Pages and pages of waivers.

"If you choose to join Club Reverie, you will have access to our program twice a week. No more. Should we suspect that an unhealthy attachment is beginning, you will be barred from the program until our on-staff psychologist deems you fit to return. The opportunity we are offering is not to be taken lightly; the experiences you will undergo will, for all intents and purposes, be real.

There is no risk of death or true bodily harm—though, if you choose to jump off a cliff or otherwise engage in painful activities, your body will feel some soreness once you exit the program—but even so, the psychological ramifications of something like this are delicate, and we take no chances when it comes to the wellbeing of our clients." Devyn points to the tablet. "If you are still interested, we can discuss the further details, payment and such—"

"I'm in."

She pulls back, startled, but her eyes sparkle. "You don't want time to consider? The possibility of such an undertaking can be immense to some—"

"I'm in." I'm already flying through the pages on the tablet, signing here, initialing there. I barely even read it. Something about the monthly cost flashes by me; eh, I'll figure it out.

Because this.

This is worth it.

This is everything.

I'll get to be in Fort Precipice. Walking the halls of the Night Court.

I'll get to see, feel, hear, *touch* Kilian.

Kilian.

My hand is shaking by the time I'm done signing. Eagerness, nervousness, terror, excitement—just, *everything.*

After a quick session of Devyn fitting me to the headset, she sits on a small stool next to me, the tablet in her lap.

"Are you ready, Sloane?" she asks, and all that nervous energy buzzes electric and alive in my chest. I haven't felt this *much* in a long, long time.

I haven't felt this *alive* in a long, long time.

"Oh, I'm ready," I tell her. "So...you'll drop me at the beginning of...of *that* scene?" I choke. "And you'll be *sitting here* the whole time? Won't you hear...um..."

Okay this whole thing suddenly got super weird. Maybe I should have thought it through a bit—

Devyn laughs and bats her hand at the glass wall. "That's the purpose of the windows. Once you're in the program, I will leave, and the windows will be darkened for privacy. We set the time of your excursion to a specific length—to start, one hour. You will be gently ejected from the program at that mark, unless you wish to exit sooner, in which case, you need only touch the spot on the back of your neck. It connects to the helmet and will draw you out of the fantasy. There are staff who monitor your vitals for any oddities, but you will be in a world all your own."

Okay. Okay, that's not so bad.

But my nerves are in high gear again, my pulse thudding heavily in my wrists, my throat.

I give Devyn a nod and lean back on the chair. "All right. I'm ready. Do I—"

Devyn smiles. "What specifically attracted you to Club Reverie? If you don't mind my asking."

My mouth goes dry. I brace for an onslaught of my usual embarrassment over how powerfully my inner response is, how desperately I want what she's offering—how desperately I wanted it even when it was just a vague idea on a flier. But in her stare, all I feel is comfort. Like she understands the gnawing need that's taken over my waking hours. Like maybe she spends every free moment lost in fantasy too.

"'Your favorite fictional worlds become real,'" I echo the flier. "'Reality has no limitations.'"

Devyn's grin softens. She stares at me for a moment longer, that analysis back in her eyes—what is she looking for?—before she turns her focus to the tablet.

"You're definitely in the right place, Sloane," she tells me. "Just relax and enjoy."

My eyelids flutter shut as a soft whirring fills my brain, rattling through my head like a dozen hummingbirds—and before I can ask anything else, before I can take another fortifying breath, I blink.

And I'm standing in the central hall of Fort Precipice.

The throne room. The heavy, dark black walls with faintest pinpricks of candlelight. The embroidered runner leading from me, all the way to—

To—

Holy *fuck*.

Holy fuckity *fuck*.

Kilian.

Kilian Kilnmor.

He's my fantasy but better, the image I conjured of him but hewed, softened, enhanced. Black hair, those bright eyes, that domineering presence, every description from the book made real. He's even in the same position as the book, leaning forward on his throne in a stifled rage—

Which means.

This is that scene.

That scene.

I take a step forward, because Isaura did, because she walked down this runner. The moment I do, I feel the fabric brush my legs, and when I look, I see *that* dress. Only—*my god*, my imagination never made anything like *this*, twisting bands of glittering gold and silver that braid across my torso, barely covering my breasts, showing a diamond cut out over my stomach, long slits in the skirts letting my bare legs peek through. The gown is described as *sin* in the book, but holy shit, this more than lives up to it.

I'm so shocked by this gown that I only note after a beat that this is, in fact, *my* body. I'm not in some version of Isaura—this is my hair hanging down in curls around me, styled and soft, my skin showing through the cut outs in the fabric, my not-exactly-impressive breasts pushed high beneath this fabric.

My normal wardrobe alternates from comfortable clothes to work attire, and yeah, I always salivated over Isaura's clothing—but to actually be *wearing* a dress like this. And to not only wear it, but to *feel* myself in it, an unseen wave of sexiness and power pulsing through me.

I may not be Isaura, but I feel like a queen all the same.

"You dare come here," Kilian's voice booms, "alone and unarmed. Did you think you would be welcomed?"

My whole body flares to life under the touch of his voice.

I can feel the reverberations of his anger. I can taste the candle smoke on the air. I can see him, his fury, his coiled tension.

I walk, and keep walking, tears pricking my eyes, more afraid than ever that I'll wake up.

So afraid I'll wake up that I totally miss saying Isaura's line.

Kilian stands before he's supposed to. "You show yourself before me, and you have nothing to say for what you have done?"

Oh, shit.

This is—not the book.

Crap crap shit. What did Devyn say? I could play this as Isaura, but I could also make my own choices, take the narrative in my own direction—

Kilian lifts a hand and flicks his wrist. *Shit*, I recognize that motion—everyone in the fandom knows that motion—he's casting a spell. He's summoning his guards.

Terror cuts through me. In the book, the guards come, but later—once Kilian and Isaura are already, well…

"Wait!" I gasp. "Wait—Kilian, I—"

Isaura. What would Isaura say? What *did* she say? That line—about not wanting welcome—

But I'm not Isaura. I never wanted to be.

I wanted to be Sloane. With him.

And this is my chance.

CHAPTER 4: KILIAN

The last time I was with her was a mistake. I should not even be giving her moments to speak at all—that is weakness, weakness I allowed to go too far last time. Hers is not the only kingdom that would love nothing more than to claim Precipice as their own; I cannot lose sight of all I have accomplished, all I have to lose.

She has laid this trap, and I may have willingly walked into it last time, but no more.

She is halfway to my throne when I flare my wings out, filling the room from wall to wall. It stops her short, her eyes widening; I catch the quick rise and fall of her chest.

How dare she dress her body in a gown such as that, a sumptuous gift, begging to be unwrapped? She knows precisely each move she makes. Is that how she slipped past my guards, by using her wiles to distract them while she cast her spells?

As if they could hear my thoughts touch on them, behind her, the doors to the throne room slam open. My guards stream in, half a dozen of them pulled by my summons, all as equally imposing as the figure I cut. They surround her instantly, a perfect, choreographed circle of winged Precipice warriors, each man holding a spear or sword at the ready, their angled wings ranging from onyx to shadow gray. They know to take no chances with one such as her.

I will deal with their shortcomings later. However they allowed her to pass, she is here now.

"Kilian," she gasps, her wide eyes darting to each of my warriors. When she looks back up at me, her shoulders deflate, terror for outright worry. She has lost something, or worries she is losing it.

I ignore the similar twist in my own chest. Memories of our last encounter fight to be at the front of my mind—the way her body felt beneath my fingers, the taste of her honeyed sweetness—

"Broderick," I growl the guard captain's name. "Use the magic-dampening manacles."

"Sir." My brother moves to obey with the practiced air of loyalty and dedication.

The manacles clack as he nears her, and she flinches back from him, a terror in her that I did not think her capable of.

"Wait—Kilian! Just—hear me out! I promise, I don't—"

"Your words are poison, Sloane."

The look on her face stuns me to silence.

All her terror, all her worry, all her panic—

it vanishes immediately. There is only awe, and in this moment between us, I feel a deep rip in my chest.

The memories of our first time together congeal, and I see her clearly, a fast, heady pulse of her that has my mouth salivating, my cock hardening. I have had her, I know I have, and yet something winds tight in my gut, a hunger as though I need to know what she tastes like.

The way she is watching me now, her face ripe with her own longing, the tenderness of her name in my mouth—I am lucky the room is filled with my guards. I am lucky she is still at least three paces from me, too far to touch.

"Take her to the dungeon," I manage, but I am drowning in her watery eyes.

Broderick snaps the manacles on her. I heave relief, but the emotions do not drop—whatever I feel is mine alone, not an illusion cast by her.

Self-hatred flares. It redirects when Sloane makes the smallest, softest whimper in her throat, and I fume, my wings still extended, lifting, cutting her into shadow.

"I will interrogate the Dawn Queen personally," I snarl.

CHAPTER 5: SLOANE

If I'm being perfectly honest, this is about as good as I expected something like this to go. I get my chance to actually live out my wildest fantasy, and I fucking *blow it* by doing *literally nothing.*

Though, I mean, being handcuffed in the center of six Precipice warriors isn't the worst thing in the world. I see the way they all look at me, their eyes heavy with lust that they keep restrained only because of the silent yet wrathful High Prince storming up the hall ahead of us, and *wow* is that empowering. And erotic. The warriors are described just as decadently sexy as Kilian in the book, and Club Reverie is totally nailing these depictions of them.

I bite my lip, my eyes flitting from warrior to warrior—I guess each of them from the book, five of Kilian's closest childhood friends and one of his brothers.

A shiver runs up my spine, but we've reached the dungeon by now.

And I realize I have no idea what's going to happen, because this wasn't in the book.

My breathing is tight and uneven, my heartbeat racing like crazy as Kilian himself yanks open a barred cell door.

"In," he commands, and while part of me still wants to resist and explain myself out of this, a stronger part of me walks right past the guards and enters the cell.

Kilian's eyes don't leave mine the whole while. A muscle tics in his forehead when I obey, and I think I see a flash of a smile that he quickly recorrects.

"Await my further instructions up the hall," he tells his guards without looking away from me.

I stay motionless in the middle of the cell as the guards file out. One lingers—I don't even have to look to know it's Broderick, Kilian's next oldest brother—but the moment they're gone, Kilian moves.

He's fast, silent, deadly, and I have no time to react before he grabs the chain between the manacles and yanks it up, up, high over my head, so my toes leave the ground and I'm dangling face-level with him. I gasp at the shock of being lifted, but more at the shock of being suddenly so close to him.

So very fucking close to him.

There's a wall sconce in the hall, and that unsteady orange light is all we have to illuminate the space between us. It cuts geometric patterns in the sharp lines of his face, making him look even wilder, even more lethal.

"Tell me why you have come," he demands.

I squirm in his grip, wrists pulling painfully against the iron. "I came—" Fuck, Sloane, *think* for a second before you ruin this even more. "I came because—"

My thoughts go completely blank. Blank except for every *real* excuse, that hey I found this club that's letting me live out my fantasy with you because I'm fucking pathetic and would rather live in fiction than reality—

Kilian walks me backward. Something rattles, then he pulls away, leaving me chained with my hands over my head, my spine to the cold stone wall.

"I came because I had to see you." It bursts out of me.

He turns his back to me, his head tipping to the side so I see him in profile. "You have thanked me already." His tone is carefully level. Carefully emotionless.

My mind rattles. Thanked him—

Oh. *Right.*

Isaura and Kilian recently fucked for the first time—after he saved her from Ambrose, another High Prince of a different kingdom that stands as an enemy of both Precipice and the Dawn Queen. Kilian visited Ambrose under the pretense of negotiating peace while his men scouted for Ambrose's weaknesses; they found it, when they uncovered the Dawn Queen in his court, given over to him as a marriage pawn by her traitorous mother.

Kilian freed her, only for himself and Isaura to barely escape capture, hiding in the scraggly cliffs that border Kilian and Ambrose's nations.

Alone but for each other, certain they would be captured at any moment, Kilian and Isaura gave into their lust and survival fears in a moment mutual panic.

"I did not come for more...thanks," I say lamely. "I came because...because I'm weak."

It bursts out of me. Pinched. Aching. Too truthful.

Kilian Kilnmor, my fantasy made real, pauses.

He turns to look at me. "You are far from weak, Dawn Queen."

"No." I pull against the chained manacles, my toes barely touching the floor. "I'm not. I came for the sole reason of seeing you. And that makes me weak."

Fuck these tears in my eyes, really.

Kilian appraises me for a long moment. And when his eyes leave my face to run lazily down my body, that tingle of need between my legs flares again.

That's desire in his eyes.

And I'm not imagining the way his pants are

tenting.

Oh my god. Oh my *god*.

Excited panic sends my mind into a white snowstorm, but I grip my hands into fists, grounding myself.

None of this is real, my mind whispers. *He's a program. Of course he's attracted to you; it's how he's coded.*

But the rest of me thrashes against that reasoning. This feels *so* real. Everything, down to the way my body strains from being chained up, to the smell of this prison cell, tangy iron and dampness. And Kilian—he's as real as Eden and Kyle were at Jacked Up.

None of this is real, my mind whispers again, but I ignore it.

"You—you wanted to see me, too," I guess.

I can see the answer in his eyes.

The edges tighten. His pupils dilate.

I pull against the manacles again, fighting to close the foot of space between us. If I could just touch him—if I could just—

Kilian chuckles, rumbling deep and dark in his chest. "Watching you struggle is sweet. I did not think you capable of losing your composure."

I relent against the manacles and give him a sardonic glare. "And I did not think you capable of behaving so barbarically as to chain up a woman."

Barbaric. The word he used to describe

Ambrose after he rescued Isaura.

He lunges, hand going to my throat, pinning me to the wall.

The moan I release is all need, choking and thick, and I know he hears it in the way he cuts his tongue across his lips.

"Do not compare me to *him*," he speaks evenly, barely restrained. "And you are not a woman, Dawn Queen. Even then, in the cliffs, you were as you are now: my enemy. Particularly when you arrive in *my* court uninvited. Did you think our time together changed our relationship?"

Isaura would deny it.

But my lips part. "Yes."

He's so close now. He smells of warm, sharp spices that infuse my senses, dizzying me. His body presses to mine, corded muscle, his long, hard cock wedged between us.

"Yes," I say again, louder. "It changed me. I am not your enemy—right now, Night Prince, I am merely yours entirely."

Finally, I say the right thing.

Kilian claims my mouth with all the force of who he is. Everything he does is deliberate and orchestrated; so when he breaks, it is vigorous, and I get swept up in it.

His kiss is a thunderstorm, all of me consumed in a battering of sensation. The relentless, demanding thrashes of his tongue inside my mouth; the tight pinching grip of his hand on my neck; the soft fullness of his lips. I open myself to him, my body a fireworks display of electricity and joy.

He pulls back, just a breath of space, and puts his thumb on my lower lip. "You should know by now the reception enemies receive in my court."

I grin, body slack against the chains. "You greet all enemies like this?"

Kilian laughs. God, that sound—it shakes through every part of my body so I go even more pliant.

He bends back to me, his lips nipping across my mouth, my cheek, dipping down my neck. His teeth graze the skin there and I gasp, chest heaving toward him.

"Only you," he says into my shoulder. "This is how only you are received."

He lowers before me, dragging his face to every patch of skin showing through the twisting straps of this dress. I throw my head against the wall, unable to speak past the way he stops to press a kiss to the fabric that covers my breast, his mouth opening, tongue flicking hard enough that I feel it zip through my nipple.

The gasp I let loose is senseless and wild; I'm coming undone.

"Stay silent, Sloane," he orders into my

other breast, and this time, he grabs the fabric and yanks it down, baring me to him.

My teeth dig into my lip, burrowing hard to contain myself. The need to obey him is ingrained and dominating; he may be the one slowly lowering to his knees, but I'm at his mercy.

He holds, motionless, until I look down at him, already in a heady fog. Only once my eyes find his does he move, slowly, *slowly* drawing my pebbled nipple into his mouth.

I croon into my pinched lips as he sucks, his teeth gently clamping down until I hiss in shock. It's been so long since I've even been close to a situation like this, touched by someone other than my own hands and toys, that this alone would be enough to drive me over the edge; but the fact that it's *Kilian Kilnmor*, and I can *feel him*—

My vision starts to waver, black spots gliding across my eyes, but dammit, *I will not pass out.*

He chuckles, the sound vibrating across my skin, and delves lower.

"Kilian—" I pant his name, half to keep from screaming, half to orient my brain in this moment. This is happening. This is—

He drops to his knees and wastes no time— my dress parts easily in his deft hands and he loops one of my thighs over his shoulder.

I watch him, stunned, all my body sparking

with sensation—one touch from him, and I'll be an eruption.

But he strokes his fingers gently through my curled hair, his face breaking in something mournful, something soft. "I have thought of you every moment since we parted," he says, his eyes lifting to mine. "I have dreamed of your taste, of the sounds you make. Until this moment—" he eyes the magic-dampening manacles "—I thought my emotions some spell you had cast on me. But they persist, though your powers are controlled. And so I know that I alone am to blame for how deliriously I want to feel you come apart on my tongue again."

Holy shit holy shit holy—

He dives in, and I clamp my teeth together, head throwing back, every focus pinned on not coming, not yet, fucking hell *not yet*. He's an expert though, and I know I'm not strong enough to fight it off for long.

Kilian uses his thumbs to spread me wide, the cold dungeon air throwing an initial shiver through me; he rides that wave and runs a long, languid lick through my pussy, delving deep inside, probing my heat. I writhe against him, needing deeper, needing more. He ignores my strangled pleas, taking his time just playing with his tongue, tasting me, licking here, there.

"Why did you come?" he asks between

torments. "Why did you come to Fort Precipice so very vulnerable, my lady?"

This is a tangled web—we want each other, badly, but he is still my enemy, and I am now his prisoner. I feel that to my core in this moment, the way I'm manacled to the wall, the sheer strength and domination in his every movement.

By the moans of pleasure I hear reverberating in his throat, I know he's enjoying this on his own—but this is a form of torture, a skilled unwinding of my last defenses; I'm sweating, fevered, unwound.

"I needed you," I say, the honest truth. "I need—Kilian—*please*—"

"Mm, yes, beg for me," he rumbles. "Beg, and I may be lenient."

Kilian drags his tongue out of my slit and swirls it around my clit. Again. Again. He draws circle after circle, not yet touching the one spot I need to unleash, and I thrash against the manacles, wishing I could grab his head, direct him where I need him to go.

"Kilian—" His name from me is a pathetic, blubbering plea. He knows he has me there, right on the edge. It's a dance, a game, and he is winning.

Kilian looks up at me, waits until I lock eyes with him, then clamps his lips around my clitoris and sucks, *hard*.

I come apart with a piercing shriek that I only think to dampen at the last moment, screaming into my pinched lips as my body shreds and reknits itself in the span of seconds. Stars buzz and lights flash; still, he doesn't relent, demanding every last ounce of pleasure out of my body until I shudder and collapse, dangling from the chains, utterly drained.

Kilian rises up, wiping my juices off his chin with the back of his hand. He rolls his eyes shut in his own ecstasy, and I damn near come again just by the look on his face—that he could get so much pleasure from my orgasm.

"This session was to sate my own fire," Kilian says. "Going forward, you will find me a much less hasty interrogator. I am surprised by how quickly your defenses crumbled, Sloane darling. I will give you time to regain your composure."

Blearily, I get my eyes to focus on him. He dips back in for another soul-wrenching kiss, his hand squeezing hard on my throat.

Then he's gone, walking fast to the door.

"Kilian." I tug against the chain. It's still locked tight. "Kilian—you can't leave me here!"

Panic sets in again. Because this is exactly what Kilian Kilnmor would do.

He closes the cell door behind him and peers in it at me, reading the confusion on my face.

His eyes trail to my exposed breast, the way my gown is still thrown over one leg, and a spark of appreciation has him arching a brow.

"You are the loveliest addition to my dungeon," he says. "I don't know why I didn't think of keeping you down here sooner."

"Kilian!"

"I'll be back tomorrow, Sloane. We'll continue our interrogation then."

"*Kilian!*"

He walks away without another word. And even though I thrash helplessly against the manacles, even though I'm left exposed and vulnerable in the dark, I'm smiling like the absolute idiot I am, and I don't think I'll ever be able to stop.

CHAPTER 6: SLOANE

Not five minutes later, the program spits me out, and I blink into the dim lighting of my room at Club Reverie. It's lucky that my time limit was up in only an hour—I was manacled to a fucking wall and couldn't very well reach the spot on the back of my neck to eject myself early. What a waste it'd have been to spend hours just hanging there—but actually, some people get off on that sort of kink, don't they? Either way, I'll have to ask Devyn about a different exit strategy, in case Kilian makes a habit of chaining me up.

I grin as the helmet whirs around me and retracts on its own, sliding up and into the ceiling, out of sight. I swing my legs over the side of the chair, my body thrumming still, tender and relaxed, feeling everything that happened—

—even though none of it *did* happen.

My joy immediately deflates, a balloon hissing out air.

It was easier to ignore that fact in the program. Now, my eyes trail around the small room, seeing the details but not really focusing, and every ounce of pleasure still camped in my body starts to sour.

I want back in.

I want back in so badly that tears prick my eyes. I scrub them away, fast, just in case Devyn lied and someone is watching me—I can't let them think I'm already developing an unhealthy obsession.

In truth, it's way too late for that.

This is everything I've ever wanted. But knowing that it isn't real clashes with just how fantastically happy this experience made me. How can something fake feel this *right*? How can something that doesn't exist make me feel this fulfilled, this centered, this whole? I barely spent an hour with Kilian, but the connection we had— the tension—the *passion*—

My eyes land on the tablet Devyn used to set my program. *One of the more popular destinations,* she'd said.

So that means dozens of people, maybe more, have lived the exact scene that I just lived. Maybe not in the dungeon—I'm probably one of the few dumb enough to end up there—but still a moment like that, with Kilian.

I push at my chest, not really sure what this feeling is. Jealousy? Anger? Protectiveness? I should feel those things, right? Or maybe I shouldn't.

I can see now why Devyn thought I'd want to take some time to think about joining. This isn't as simple as playing a video game. This is…real.

Too real. But not real enough.

When I stand from the chair, my copy of *Fort of Night and Edge* tumbles out of my lap, along with the unopened water bottle. I grab them both, staring down at the cover of the book for so long that I damn near jump out of my skin when the door softly clicks open.

"How'd we do?" Devyn leans in with a bright smile.

Years of customer service experience is the only thing that lets me smile back at her. "Great," I say. "When can I come back?"

I shouldn't go back.

Should I?

I can't, anyway, for three days—Club Reverie policy for first timers to space out sessions. So I trudge through the rest of the night in a daze, then stumble back to work in the same fog. It doesn't abate, doesn't break.

All I can think about is seeing Kilian again. Whether I even *should* see him again. This feels like I'm feeding some sort of addiction, yet at the same time, a part of me keeps trying to rationalize the connection we'd had. But *of course* we had a connection—who would pay for an experience like that if there was no programmed connection? But can something like that really be fabricated?

These questions are too big. Especially

while I'm juggling scalding coffee beverages, and halfway through pouring shots of espresso into a cup of hot milk, I lose my grip and the whole lot goes splashing over my hand.

"Fuck me," I hiss.

Eden whirls around from the register and gives me the same concerned frown she's been giving me all shift. "Sorry," she says to the waiting customer before turning to me and whispering, "Go take your five. Or ten, maybe."

"Yeah, thanks," I say, but it comes out harsher than necessary. I'm just…on edge. And this milk burn doesn't help things.

I make my way into the back room—thankfully Kyle isn't in today—and rummage through the cupboards for the super old first aid kit stashed behind the likely expired fire extinguisher. I find a bandage, some burn cream, and manage to wrap my hand as best I can, all the while wallowing in how much of an idiot I am.

A few minutes later, Eden slips into the back room. "We've got a lull. Are you okay?"

I wave my bandaged hand at her from where I sit on one of the plastic folding chairs around the small circular kitchen table. "I'm fine. Feeling supremely stupid, but fine."

Eden takes the seat across from me. Her eyes are still narrow in that worried, analytical way. We've worked together for two years now, and I'd consider us friends, even though we don't exactly hang out after work—though, thinking about it now, that's my fault. Eden's invited me to a couple parties before. I turned her down every time.

Because I'd rather be home, reading, lost in my own world, than anywhere else.

I wince, and not because of the burn.

"You know you can talk to me, right?" Eden says slowly. "If you ever need to."

I give her a small smile. "Thanks. I—" I start to give a brush off response, but I stop myself.

Try, for once, I think, and I shift up straighter.

"I went to Club Reverie," I start, and before I can worry myself into thinking I'm being too awkward or annoying or *much*, I launch into the whole thing, from an abbreviated version of my obsession with *Night Prince and Dawn Queen*—luckily she knows about that, because that's like 90% of my personality—to the way Club Reverie works to how real the session felt. I leave out the exact details of what Kilian and I did, but by the time I'm done, I'm panting, watching Eden for any of the reactions I expect.

An eyeroll. A shrugged dismissal. Some way for her to extract herself from the conversation she now realizes is *way* too weird.

But she nods, cheek caught between her

teeth. "This isn't like a therapy tool, is it?"

An honest question. I stare for a full second, not used to people sticking around this long after I divulge so much of my personal shit. "Um, no. I mean, I didn't ask, but for my uses, no. It's purely recreational."

She nods again. "Well, it sounds to me like you're *trying* to make it some sort of therapy tool. But it's just for fun, right? It's like going to see a movie or playing laser tag or some shit. It's fun. But it doesn't sound like you had fun."

"I did," I say quickly. Because I really, honestly did. "I'm just—I don't know. It feels like there are things I need to consider and a lot of emotion involved and I don't know what to do."

"Then stop. If it's that intense, when it sounds like it's only supposed to be something you do because you enjoy it, then it's clearly not for you."

"But…I did enjoy it." I try to say that without pouting.

Eden laughs. "Then keep going! But remember that it's only for *fun*. It isn't like you're committing to a new life trajectory. You're playing a game. Remember that."

The front door chimes, and Eden hops up.

"Thank you," I say quickly.

She pauses at the door and gives me another big smile. "Of course." She nods at my hand. "But that means you're on register duty now."

I follow her up, and as I go back to work, my brain feels less jumbled.

Fun. Club Reverie is supposed to be *fun*.

I'm overthinking it. To the surprise of *no one*. I'm acting like seeing Kilian and experiencing him is something life-changing, when it doesn't have to be.

In the back of my mind, a quiet voice whispers, *Does it?*

CHAPTER 7: KILIAN

The Dawn Queen's forces have not moved or retaliated, so likely they do not know I hold her captive in my dungeon—or else she is planning something greater I cannot see.

I am grateful for the other issues that demand my attention the days after her capture. The list of countries that Precipice can call ally is short, and much of the meetings I find myself in deal with the myriad of rival kingdoms and their movements against each other as well as me. Webs weave through them all, tangled and ever expanding—lies told, treaties overturned, magicians and mages who play with fates like a game of cards.

The breadth of the pieces set against my land leaves a pulsing twinge at the base of my skull.

"Headache?" Broderick walks alongside me as we leave a meeting with couriers from generals stationed on my eastern border.

"Always," I moan, rubbing at the knot.

Broderick casts his hand over the spot I knead, and in an instant, the pain is gone.

I lift my eyebrow. "Your skills at healing are improving."

He shrugs. "It's Micah. He's been teaching all the guards minor healing spells."

"If our brother is more inclined towards that route, he should be in the infirmaries, not the barracks. I'll reassign him."

"Ah, wait on that," Broderick says with a mischievous grin. "He's having fun with his current assignment."

I frown, thinking—

Then I come to hard stop in the middle of the hall.

My youngest brother is one of the guards I entrusted to care for Sloane—to let her down from the wall, but not to undo the magic dampening manacles; to give her food and water; and to not *touch* her.

The glare of fury I pin on Broderick could wither a weaker soul.

"My instructions were explicit," I state. "What precisely is Micah *enjoying*?"

Broderick casts a look up at me.

He and a handful of my men know the nature of my interactions with Sloane. Does he guess that this is no longer a game of power, but that something true blossoms beneath the strategy?

Even thinking that question leaves me reeling within myself.

I have not dared to admit that I am no longer able to compartmentalize the acts I have done to her from my feelings for her. I have thought about her body chained in my dungeon every moment of every day since; I have relived the memory of her cunt on my tongue in the darkness of my room, my cock rigid in my own fist; I have pictured her perfect moans and her delicious whimpers and the fire in her eyes when she sparred verbally with me.

She and I have done far more than that moment in the dungeon. I have been inside of her, thrusting and unbound; and yet the memory of the dungeon burns the brightest.

It is consuming me. Second by second.

Broderick shakes his head. "No one has touched her, High Prince. I merely meant that Micah has enjoyed seeing our enemy brought low. We all have. It is cause for rejoicing, is it not?"

That does nothing to abate my fury.

But it should.

The Dawn Queen is one of Precipice's greatest enemies. Seeing her imprisoned, shamed, is a right of all here, especially the men who have fought her soldiers on battlefields, who have lost friends, brothers, family to the torrent that is her army.

Freeing her from Ambrose was not about Sloane—it was to shame Ambrose, to weaken him, because I knew the Dawn Queen was not there of her own will. And I guessed correctly—freeing her allowed her to return to her kingdom, unseat her faithless mother, and turn her armies away from supporting Ambrose. That urchin is left now with not a single ally.

That the Dawn Queen was grateful for my assistance was a mere bonus.

That she and I found ourselves alone in the mountains after...

She is my enemy, I tell myself. *She is Precipice's enemy.*

I should not feel this lurch of protectiveness at the thought of my men leering at her.

She is my enemy, I think again. *MY enemy. It is I alone who claims this power over her.*

"Have her brought to my room," I tell Broderick as I walk away. I cannot let him see the truth in my face.

"Sir?"

I do not repeat myself.

CHAPTER 8: SLOANE

"All right." Devyn pulls the tablet into her lap and starts typing away. "The emergency exit now will be to squeeze your left palm twice—my apologies; few of our first timers find themselves in situations that negate being able to tap the back of your neck."

Devyn doesn't give me time to feel embarrassed—nothing about her tone is accusatory, either, merely polite conversation. She has that aura about her, the ability to immediately put people at ease, and fuck, it's the complete opposite of who I am.

"And," she continues, "since you wish to continue the story you began, you will be placed in the next scene with Kilian—which will be...ah, you will be brought to his room in chains from the dungeon, where you have been held for three days."

"Three days?" I chirp. I'm already sitting back on the chair, but that detail has me bolting upright. "He left me in the cell for *three days?*"

Devyn gives a sly grin. "He is not a hero, Sloane. This is where he is taking the story."

"Yeah, yeah—wait, where *he* is taking the

story?"

Does she pause? But Devyn's smile doesn't waver. "Where his character is taking the story based on the choices you made."

Well, that makes sense. This is exactly what Kilian Kilnmor would do to Isaura—leave her stewing for days while he fought to deny his feelings for her. But I'm still upset. I feel like he *has* left me stewing for three days, in a way, because I've spent so much time wanting to be back here, counting the minutes, all the while trying to convince myself that it's *just for fun* and nothing else.

But all this is really self-inflicted worry and I have nothing to be mad at him for. Right? Right.

So when the headset lowers and Devyn leaves the room, I close my eyes, and I feel exactly like a dangerous queen who has been locked away at the whim of her enemy.

Well. Sort of.

It's all fantasy, right?

This isn't real. It's just for fun.

This isn't real—

I open my eyes to darkness. The sound of keys rattling makes my head swivel to the door. I'm sitting on a bench at the back of the room—at least someone let me down from the wall

While I was half naked.

That's great.

A blush heats my cheeks as the cell door swings open.

There stands Broderick Kilnmor.

"The High Prince has requested your audience," he tells me. The disgust in his voice is unmistakable; but to him, I'm one of the people responsible for the suffering of his kingdom. It's earned. "You will come easily and without struggle."

I stand slowly. I must have been given clothes to change into; my sparkly gown is gone, swapped for a simple blue linen dress and flat brown shoes. I doubt I've been able to bathe in these three days, either, and I feel grimy all of a sudden, especially when I reach up to smooth my hair that's been braided back.

But still, I stand tall, because Isaura would. Because I'm here, and I will play this role, and I will *enjoy it*, fuck me.

Broderick scowls as he gestures for me to walk ahead of him. The manacles clank between my wrists as I go slowly, letting his grunts of direction lead me up through the dungeon—but not back through the main halls of the palace. Of course not. I'm a dangerous prisoner.

Instead, Broderick corrals me through narrow, dark staircases, the air tinged with iron and moist stone, up, up, up through the fort, until we reach a heavy closed door.

He knocks, and a beat later, opens the door. Inside is Kilian's bedchamber.

My whole body seizes, hands in fists, stomach winding tight, thighs pressing together. There's the massive canopy bed where Kilian and Isaura eventually wile away days after signing the peace treaty between their two nations; there's the towering hearth even now housing a roaring fire where Kilian burned that same peace treaty after Isaura later tried to kill him, before he knew she was cursed to.

My head is swimming so much with all the overlapping scenes from these books that I nearly miss the dark presence that rises from one of the heavy mahogany chairs near the flames.

I'm drawn to him, siting him like he's the only thing here. And he is; everything else fades as my eyes connect with Kilian's, and that tension in my body only winds tighter.

"Thank you, Broderick," Kilian says. "You may leave us."

Broderick hesitates. In the book, he doesn't approve of his brother's relationship with Isaura, but he comes around; it's that displeasure I feel burn into the side of my face now as Broderick glares at me, then leaves down the same staircase we entered.

The door shuts behind me with a click.

"Your countrymen have not rallied to your

rescue," Kilian starts. He turns his gaze to the fire, his demeanor more relaxed than I've seen yet. There's still an air of strain to him, but his arms are slack at his sides, his jaw unclenched, the top buttons of his shirt undone. I can't guess the time, but by the darkness beyond the glass panes across from me, I'd say it was nearly dusk.

He must have been getting ready for bed. Winding down after a long day.

I take a step forward. "No. They won't."

And it isn't a lie. Isaura's country doesn't rise to her aid both because she doesn't need them to and because she really was trying to broker peace when she came. Of course, her peace intentions were poisoned by her own curse to kill him, but still.

Kilian looks up at me with a flicker of surprise. "No? What reason did you have to hand yourself over to me then, if not to stage yet another battle between us?"

This is almost an identical conversation from the book. Different setting, but the words flow; Isaura's, not mine. It helps to say what she said. All I want to do is fall blubbering to my knees, tell Kilian that none of this is real and I'm trying to enjoy it but it's killing me that it's fake. Isaura, though, has only strategy on her mind.

She's stronger than I am.

"Peace," I say and take another step. "I want

peace, Kilian. This has gone on too long. I cannot weather more death. I cannot weather more bloodshed. I cannot—" My breath catches. "I cannot weather another day apart from you."

It's the truth, from both Isaura and me, and saying the words makes my stomach squeeze, lurching me forward another step so I'm close enough to reach out and touch Kilian. If I could. The manacles are cold and heavy, my wrists chafing—I could do without the realism touch, thanks, Devyn—and I let my earnest show.

Kilian frowns at me, but he doesn't retreat at my advancing.

"You don't trust me," I say.

You shouldn't, I want to add, but I swallow the wince.

This isn't real. It's just for fun.

I lift the magic-dampening manacles. "But you know I am not bewitching you. I will prove my truth to you."

"While my prisoner?" Kilian's eyebrow lifts. "You are many things, Sloane, but what talents will you employ to prove you speak the truth while you are in a position with nothing to lose? Desperation to be free motivates you more than a sudden change of heart."

"Sudden?" I take another step. "Yes. You changed me quite suddenly. All at once."

God, I feel even filthier now next to him;

he's utterly pristine, his dark hair oiled and set back against his head, his skin smelling of those sharp spices. What do I smell like? I don't even want to go down that road.

So I do the only thing I can think to do, and it isn't even something Isaura did—

I mimic him in the dungeon, and I kneel before him.

He doesn't move, but I can feel his presence change; moderately relaxed to immediately alert. His wings flicker out, once, before cinching up tight against his back.

Face level with his crotch, I see his cock growing hard through his pants.

I lift my hands and work at the bindings around his waist. God, how long has it been since I sucked a guy off? And I never got what you'd call *good feedback* from the few I was with, which suddenly makes my hands shake, the chain rattling embarrassingly.

Kilian snatches my hands.

I sip in a breath and go perfectly still.

He reaches forward to cup my jaw in one hand, running his thumb along my lower lip, and when I manage to look up at him, he's backlit by the fire so I see mostly shadow, only the flash and spark of his eyes catching mine.

Steadiness rises through me.

With his hands on mine, I undo the ties on

his pants and pull him free.

His cock bobs before me, even more massive than I'd dared imagine, long and thick, the tip glistening.

When he'd knelt at my feet in the dungeon, I'd felt excitement bordering on combustion.

Now, I feel a settling, centering kind of awe.

I grab the base of his cock and run my tongue up the side. I know now how he was able to take so much pleasure from my own pleasure; just getting to do that, *taste* him, has my eyes rolling back, my pussy spasming with need. The heady musk of him draws a whimper from my throat that I do nothing to hide.

He's silent above me. So silent I worry maybe I'm not doing it right, maybe I should be doing it faster—

His hand goes to my jaw again, calm, soft touches that settle my thoughts without a word.

"I will prove that all I want is peace," I say to the tip of his cock. My eyes flick up to his— what I can see of his face in the shadows is strained, the whole of his focus on me.

I glide my mouth around him in one quick shove.

"I know of spies in your court from other nations," I say when I pull back.

Again, taking him slowly, deeper this time.

"I will give you lists. Names, their associates, their plans."

Again, deeper, pausing when my eyes start to water, willing my throat to relax.

I make a pattern of it—pulling back long enough to list the names that Isaura listed in the book. Traitors she willingly turned over because they were from other nations and of little consequence to her; but some spies, too, that she herself bought off within Kilian's own court.

One name stays in the back of my mind. One name that she didn't give—because she didn't know he was a traitor at the time. But I know, because I'm not Isaura; what would happen if I told Kilian now of the biggest enemy in his court?

After the fifth name, though, Kilian grabs the sides of my head, holding my mouth around him. I can hear him panting, subtle yet grating gasps for composure.

I hum around him and he hisses before pulling my head off, freeing himself from my mouth. When I try to go back in, he takes a wide step away and reaches down to grab the manacles.

"But I—" I barely get a protest out before he's hauling me, bodily, across the room—to his bed. I go sprawling over the embroidered quilt, a mess of spread legs and rumbled skirts and my hair falling free from the braid, spewing around me in a curled cloud of darkness.

Kilian stops at the edge. "You play a dangerous game, my lady." His voice is rough, breathless, and the fact that I did that to him shoots a thrill through me. "Any of those nations you listed would gladly see you executed for the information you have given me. I could use you to buy peace with them while disposing of the Dawn Queen in one simple move. Give me one reason why I should let you live."

My heart sputters, pulse beating so loud in my ears that I barely hear my own gasping breath. I can still taste him on my tongue, salty and rich, and his cock hangs out of his pants, hard, unfulfilled.

I push up onto my elbows, too aware of my chest rising and falling, of the way Kilian has his hands in balled fists, of the heat of the fire drawing sweat in beads down my spine.

"One reason——" In the book, Isaura launched into a sweeping monologue about how he had transformed her, how she couldn't live without him.

But I am not Isaura.

Not now.

"Because I love you," is all I say.

Kilian holds, eyes darting across my face, waiting for the falter, the trip, the reveal.

But I am all earnestness. I love him. I've loved him from the moment I first read these books. I've loved him more than I admitted to myself because it was always *wrong* and *foolish* and a myriad of other reasons all culminating in the fact that *he isn't real*.

This isn't real. It's just for fun.

Tears prick my eyes. I have to look away from him, unable to hold his gaze with this sudden well of shame pulsing through me.

Get it together, Sloane. This isn't real. It's just for fun.

But it is real.

It's real to me.

He's real to me.

And it's breaking my heart.

The bed sinks in front of me and I realize I'm crying. I try to scrub the tears off my cheeks, but Kilian grabs the chain between my manacles and pulls my hands down. With his other hand, he takes my chin and turns me to face him.

He's sitting in front of me, one leg curled under him, staring at me with such an intense look of pain that I'm stricken silent.

Another tear trickles down my face and he catches it on his thumb. "This weight you bear," he starts. "You have born it too long."

"I caused this weight," I say. Isaura never talked to him like this, blubbering and raw. "I deserve to bear it alone."

One corner of Kilian's lips tips upward, a sad smile. "The same words spin circles in my head." His smile fades. "That is what first drew me to you. Like calling to like."

He means Isaura, though. He means scenes that happened before I entered this program.

My chest aches.

"None of this is real," I say, and hearing the words aloud has me gasping in panic. Will the program push me out? What happens if I say that?

But nothing changes. Kilian's eyes keep steady on my face, patient and kind, and I lean closer to him, drawn to him, unable to muster strength to stay away.

"It felt as such," he whispers, the breath of his words brushing against my lips. "I felt as in a dream—until you appeared in my court. Until I saw you standing in my throne room, a vision from both my nightmares and dreams. I had never seen such emotion so easily discerned as I did on your face. You bared yourself to me, your terror and hope; in one look, you were truer to me than my most loyal of supporters."

My eyelashes flutter. He never says anything like that to Isaura in the book. He's usually stoic and guarded, not one to effuse poetic until the very end, the last lingering pages that left the fandom staggering.

I shake my head and he moves to hold my neck as though he could stop my protest. "I'm not true, Kilian. There's so much I can't tell you—"

"I know." He squeezes my neck gently. "There is much still you do not know about me as well. But I think, over time, we can come to a place where we are fully known to each other."

I want that. I want it so badly, and I believe the sincerity in his eyes so much, that I kiss him.

It's softer than our kiss in the dungeon. I explore his lips, memorizing the texture of them, the taste of him, and he does the same, firelight shifting beyond my eyelids in gentle palpitations of orange and gold.

His hands go to my shoulders, find the ties at the back of my dress, and start to pull. I let him work the fabric down my arms until it bunches at the manacles, freeing my breasts between us. His hands trace delicate lines up and down my arms before he puts both hands over the manacles, says a few muttered words, and they pop off.

Kilian tosses them to the floor.

If I'm truly playing Isaura, I'd have my magic back. I didn't ask Devyn about that, what powers this program gave me; but I wait, too, for the surge of desire from the curse that Isaura experiences throughout the book, and that doesn't come either.

I move to kiss him again, my body dissolving into effervescence at the way his fingers trace patterns over the bare skin of my back. He moves down, pushing the dress off, lifting me up and pulling it free until I'm bare on his bed, the sensation so effervescent that my mind spins, all orange colors and careening stimulation and building, slick need.

Kilian kisses me again, and I grab onto him, unable to let him slip away even for a moment. Fumbling and desperate, I manage to get his shirt off—god, his chest, the product of military training from a young age, set by scars and sheened with sweat—and his wings unfold around us, fluffing the air in a delicate ripple.

That makes me chirp in a panic and I start to pull back from him. "Oh god, I must smell so bad—"

Kilian pulls my mouth back flush with his. "You are going nowhere, Sloane darling. I have waited too long to have you again; I will not be made to wait more."

He must be able to feel my grin against his lips, because he smiles too, wider when I shift to straddle him.

"Ah, that's right—you kept me locked away for three days. Some payment is due for that, I think."

I bite the delicate skin at the base of his neck.

Kilian growls, fingers clamping into my thighs, but he's still wearing his pants—when he works them off, it hits me in a wave as strong as the way he anchors around my hips.

I pull back to look at him, angled over him the way I'm straddling his legs. Our chests are pressed together, sweat-slicked and panting, and I twist my fingers into his hair, needing to hold him, to ground myself.

"Your heart is racing," he gasps, fingers braced against me. I can feel him wanting to lower me onto him, but he holds, our eyes locked, the moment fragile and ripe and...

And...*perfect*.

I press my lips to his forehead, mouth open, eyes slipping shut, and I let him lower me down, my cunt parting for the round, hard head of his cock. The noise that vibrates my throat is half moan, half whimper, all need—I tighten my grip on him against the battering of sensation.

He's so *big*.

I can't—we can't—

He lifts me slightly, pauses, then lowers me down again, taking more each time until in one sudden thrust, he's sheathed within me fully.

Full.

So full.

Pleasure is electric and wild, burning and beautiful, a strain that nudges at my last lingering wells of tension and urges them to give in. I cry out, head throwing back, and brace against him to rise up again; when I drop down, hard, Kilian grunts in his own euphoria.

He bends forward, lips dancing over my collar bone, down, catching my nipple in his mouth. He suckles as I ride him, hips rolling and thrusting, wanting more and unable to handle more but *needing* him deeper, deeper—

Kilian clings to me, and that's the only warning I get as he comes, arching his hips up into me in one powerful drive that has me screaming pleasure to the canopy above us. His hand works its way between us and he pinches my clit in his fingers as he rides the waves of his orgasm, but I'm already coming, fast and hard, driven to the edge by his pleasure and the sensation of his cock inside of me and the throbbing perfection that is this moment, that is *him*.

Breathless together, Kilian holds me on him as we both come down from the high. His wings are fully spread, moving to circle around us so we are in a world all our own.

"Sloane—I—" But words seem insufficient; he kisses me, and I melt into it, tears anew on my face that he wipes away.

And then he says it.

Something he doesn't say to Isaura until after they defeat the archmage, after their plans are all revealed, after he's struggled with whether or not he feels this way for months.

"I love you," Kilian whispers into my mouth, and I fall, fall, fall.

CHAPTER 9: KILIAN

She is my fantasies come to life.

The first time we fucked, it was just that—fucking, desperate and animalistic. But last night, and the times throughout the night when our bodies found each other across my bed, and we met in a searing clash of headiness and passion, has all been deeper in a way I had not known myself capable of feeling.

I did not lie to her when I told her that I loved her.

I do.

And I am a fool.

But for once, I allow myself to be that fool. Joy is such a fleeting thing in Fort Precipice, and as I gaze down at her sleeping in my bed, I feel I have an overabundance of it. Aside from the peace this union means, I feel a deeper purpose in it.

I have Sloane by my side now. I have something I did not know I was without, but now that she is here, I feel the piece she brings click into place, fortifying my soul.

She is my strength.

My chest flutters with a sudden desire to embody poets of old and bray my love from the rooftops. I settle for running my fingers through her hair, the strands damp from the bath I had called for her before we folded into sleep. She doesn't moan at my touch, barely stirs at all—I have worn her out completely.

Not only because of the night of exploring each other's bodies, but because of the prior days she spent in my dungeon.

A sharp spasm has me rolling quietly out of bed. I am not used to this feeling. *Guilt*, I think it is.

I will make it up to her.

Oh, will I make it up to her.

I pull a loose robe over my shoulders and creep out of my room with one last look back at her, angelic and peaceful where she curls her long body around one of my pillows.

It does not take long to find Broderick. He stands on patrol with our other brother, Micah, and two of my closest guards. All four of them turn to my approach.

Their eyes take in my robe. Only Broderick lets his annoyance show, though I know the rest feel as he does; as though I am betraying them by taking their enemy to my bed.

Ah. Their aversion to my relationship will have to be assuaged somehow.

For now, I am fixated on making Sloane understand the breadth of my feelings for her.

Though, if I am being truthful, I will not long be able to get the image of her in chains out of my mind.

I straighten, ignoring the sudden strain in my cock. "Gentlemen. We have need for a celebration."

Broderick's eyebrows shoot up. "In what way?"

"To celebrate peace," I say. "I have forged unity with the Dawn Queen. A party is in order."

The silence that falls between my men could choke a lesser prince.

I stand strong. "Is peace not worth celebrating?"

They eye each other. "Of course. My prince," says Broderick, and I cut him a withering glare.

His eyes drop from mine. All of them mimic him, in fact, avoiding eye contact, but I already know their truth.

A war tangles in my gut. Wanting—*needing*——to celebrate Sloane, to rejoice in joy; and knowing how very much my men have suffered, and how much anger they still feel towards her.

What can be done to soothe their feelings? What can be done to bridge this gap?

"It will be done, sir," Broderick manages. He turns quickly, and the rest follow, until there is only Micah eyeing me.

He never used to be so unreadable. As a child, he was effervescent, the most buoyant of us all; but lately he has been sour and cold.

War changes us all.

"Are you certain you can trust her, my prince?" Micah whispers. "She was once in the household of Ambrose. Who knows what affect he had on her? She and he both are powerful enemies of Precipice."

My eyes shoot skyward. Exhaustion creeps through my chest—how short lived is the joy I found in Sloane's embrace, how quickly crushed by this endless bid for war and outplaying dozens of other countries and enemies at every turn…

"I tire of living as though we are beset on all sides," I say, half to the ceiling, half to Micah.

Micah makes a hum of amusement deep in his throat. "We are, High Prince."

"Are we? Because I have the queen of one of our strongest enemies now proposing alliance, and such a union could offset these endless wars in a way that would bring lasting peace. Lasting peace, Micah. Can you even fathom such a thing?"

I look back down at him in time to catch the unveiled disgust on his face. As though what I propose is grotesque.

"Brother?" I question, but his expression changes for a wide smile. I blink—did I imagine that look? But he is all agreement now.

"Of course. Would that such a day would dawn," he says.

I frown. The list of names Sloane listed as traitors in my court runs through my mind—but Micah's name was not one she said. Nor Broderick. Nor any of my most trusted companions.

But I wonder, staring at Micah, what precisely changed him in this war. I wonder what meaning he carries behind these words. If he speaks the truth.

Wondering these things brings into even starker clarity the reason I have so quickly opened myself to Sloane: she is the one spot of truth in my world of lies and secrets, though I know she still holds secrets from me. I know there is much between us left in shadows.

How can someone be both a flame and the night? And yet she is. Something multifaceted in my life of endless darkness.

"I do not enter this peace lightly with the Dawn Queen. I am always vigilant, Micah," I say, and I let my voice linger heavy, telling him his loyalty is in question.

He flinches. "I will assist in overseeing the party arrangements, my prince."

He turns and follows in the wake of his comrades.

I watch until he fades from sight, my mind a churning sea of intentions and wishes, desires and regret.

CHAPTER 10: SLOANE

I wake up from that session with the dopiest grin on my face.

I leave Club Reverie with that same everlasting dopey grin on my face.

I run into Devyn on my way out, and she says something to me—asks me something, about my next session date, maybe?—but I just nod stupidly, and when I walk away, I see her shake her head with a smile that says *Ah, she didn't hear a word I said through her post-sex fog.*

But I'm too blissed out to be embarrassed. Besides, she knows that's what people do in their sessions; I'm hardly unique.

That wedges some reality into my joy.

Hardly unique.

This isn't real. It's just for fun.

I grind my teeth against the wave of reality threatening to crash down on my happiness, and hurry the few blocks to Jacked Up, head bent against a biting wind.

"Sloane. *Sloane*—shit, are you listening?"

No. Not at all.

I'm waffling between blissed out joy and

petrifying worry, and that's left me in this weird fugue state where I think I'm cleaning a table, but then I blink, and I'm halfway through making a...cappuccino? Sure, let's go with that.

I finish the drink and pass it off to Kyle at the register.

He looks at the drink.

Back up at me.

His nose curls. "I *said* they ordered an almond milk cappuccino—you used whole milk."

"Oh shit." I shake my head and survey my workspace—yep, there's the wrong jug on the counter.

The line of people behind Kyle is all that saves me from his wrath. Through gritted teeth, he goes, "Make it again," before spinning back to apologize to the customer.

Cheeks hot, I get started, doing my best to focus now.

But shit, all I can see, every time my eyes close, is Kilian.

Under me.

In me.

Touching me.

My skin feels electrified, flaring to life at the slightest brush, which leaves my cheeks perpetually hot and my body in this never-ending state of arousal. A few customers give me strange looks; can they tell? Do I have that sort of *glow* about me?

Shit, I don't know. All I know is that I'm happy.

Like really, insanely happy.

Eden comes in for her shift and I swear I hear Kyle mutter "Thank god," even within earshot of a handful of customers lingering at the tables.

That makes Eden give me an amused look as we pass each other in the breakroom. "What'd you do to earn his silent stewing wrath?"

"No clue." Gonna ignore the garbage can full of fucked up drink orders. "How are you?"

Eden blinks at me. Eyebrows up. Full surprise clear on her face. "Um. I'm good. Going to my boyfriend's concert tonight."

She has a boyfriend? I think I knew that, but something about the way she slowly ties on her apron makes me realize she's never told me about him before, and I've never asked.

I pull my jacket on, cheek caught between my teeth.

The lingering feeling of electricity on my skin, that aura of being so startling *alive*, infuses me with a different dizzying joy. I want more—of Kilian, yes, but also of…of…*life*. I feel deranged, like I finally got a taste of things my body is capable of feeling, and I don't want to stop. Not just amazing sex—but *feelings* in general, joy and power and *connection*.

I turn to Eden. "I never asked about him before. Your boyfriend. What's his name?"

A slow grin spreads across her face. "What's gotten into you?" Her smile dips into something sultry. "Or should I say, *who's* gotten into you? That Club Reverie working out, I take it?"

I huff a laugh. "I'd say so. But also...I just realized I've been kind of an ass." The easy way of putting it.

Eden laughs. "Well, his name's Thomas. And thanks for asking. Finally."

"That's deserved." I give her arm a squeeze as I pass her to leave, and she watches me go with a surprised look on her face, like she's seeing me for the first time.

I think she might be.

Two days later, I'm back at Club Reverie.

Devyn's waiting for me in the same room I've used each session now, only when she fits the helmet to me, her eyes linger on mine for a second.

"Are you enjoying your time at Club Reverie so far, Sloane?" She sits on that stool, tablet in her lap.

"Very much." I try not to sound too desperate, too overzealous, too *much*, but Devyn smiles like she sees right through my wall.

She opens her mouth to say something else when there's a knock at the door. A second later, a head pops in.

It's the guy she was with when I first saw her. The insanely attractive guy who looks like he was cut out of a magazine—perfectly smooth dark skin, ink-black hair, a whole demeanor of polished and put together.

He's got nothing on Kilian, though, and I smile at myself.

The guy looks at Devyn with a grin. "The conference call is starting, darling."

Devyn shakes her head. "Ah. I almost forgot." To me, she gives a sad smile. "We'll talk later, yes? I'd like to do a debrief over your time so far."

I nod. Really, anything to get this session started. I'll agree to whatever she wants.

Fuck, I'm addicted, aren't I?

The guy's eyes slide to me and he ducks back out, leaving a cloud of rich cologne in his wake.

Devyn stares at the closed door after he leaves.

For one beat.

Two.

"Um. Devyn?"

She jumps. Her eyelashes flutter, and when she looks at me again, it's that analyzing sweep that she uses often—here is the mind that created Club Reverie's technology. A scientist, through and through.

"Everything all right?" I jut my chin at the closed door.

Devyn smiles. "Of course. Just—" She hesitates. Another pause, and this time, unease settles in my gut. "Just remember that you're the one in control, Sloane. In your fantasy, and in your reality."

"Thanks." I shift in the chair. What's that look in her eyes? Not quite sorrow—interest? Like she's waiting for me to say something profound. "This really has helped me realize that. I think."

"Good." Devyn finally taps the screen. The helmet starts to whirr. "Then relax and have—"

The rest of what she's saying gets cut off as the room dissolves around me and I'm thrust back into my body in Fort Precipice.

I'm still in Kilian's bed, so not as much time must have passed here as it did out there. The moment I stir, I feel a body against my spine, strong arms coming around to cup me and pull me closer.

I melt. Fast and deliberate, pliant and eager.

"My lady, I thought you would sleep until the sun fell from the heavens. How are you feeling?" His voice is a resonant purr in my ears.

I grin, arching against him as I stretch, and he takes advantage of that position to slide his hand down the flat plane of my stomach, over the tufted hair between my legs. God, I'm wet already, aren't I? It's probably a perpetual state when I'm around him.

"I'm fantastic," I tell him. I loop my arm around his neck and twist until our lips meet. Fuck, the taste of him, the feel of his tongue licking against mine—yep, I'm wet and willing, and to show him, I spread my legs wide, hooking one over his thighs behind me.

A heavy shadow pulses the air over us, and I realize the darkness isn't necessarily from light; it's from his wings, draped in a warm cocoon.

I reach a hand up and run my fingers through the feathers, just like Isaura did in a rather famous scene in the second book.

Kilian shudders. A whole-body, rumbling shudder that I feel through every part of me.

I do it again. He shivers again and pulls me closer, my body flush with his so I feel every plane of his hardness, every ripple of his desire.

His laugh rumbles against my back. "You play a dangerous game. But there is business to attend to before I have breakfast."

His full hand cups my pussy and I hiss.

"Work before pleasure," I moan.

He nips at my earlobe before sitting up. "I have made arrangements while you were sleeping that involve you."

"Me?" For one beat, I forget that here, he

may call me Sloane, but I'm living Isaura's life. I'm not *Sloane, reluctant café barista*; I'm Sloane, the Dawn Queen.

I sit up, instantly alert, my brain scrambling to remember where we're at in the story.

"I have organized a ball," Kilian tells me, brushing a strand of hair over my bare shoulder. His wings peel back, showing a fire burning strong in his hearth, the windows shuttered so I can't guess the time. "To announce the peace between our two kingdoms. You will wish to send word to your court as well?"

It's a question, but all of this is a power move I remember from the book. Isaura had been *pissed* that Kilian had arranged this celebration without her knowing—he basically forced their relationship to symbolize peace, and while it did save both of their countries from further bloodshed, it would've been a less dickish move to *ask* her first.

Isaura, though, didn't call him on it, because she was keeping her own secrets from him, and still spent every waking moment warring with her cursed desire to kill him.

But I feel none of that, and I wonder if Devyn wrote that out of my story. I'm not cursed; I'm not Isaura; this is different.

So I cup Kilian's neck in my hand. "You have told your court the cause for this ball already?"

Kilian swallows. His gaze on me doesn't flicker, but I feel a wall go up around him, slowly; he has never forgotten that we play a game between us.

"Yes," he says with no pretense.

I tighten my grip on his throat. "You should have made sure my intentions align with yours before announcing it to the world."

"You made your intentions clear last night. I will not apologize for taking control."

No, and it's honestly sexy as hell that you did. I bite my lip. "Hm. A ball. I suppose I can extend the invitation to my court."

"You suppose so," he echoes, amusement in his voice.

Then his face flickers, a wince that he tries to cover by grabbing my wrist and pressing a kiss to my palm.

"What is it?" I whisper.

Isaura never pressed him. Isaura never asked about his shadows for fear that he would ask about hers.

It's as though he can feel the differences between his original narrative and my choices. He looks up at me, frozen in a moment of awe-induced surprise, before he strokes his thumb along my wrist.

"It is my own court I worry for," he tells me. "They are not so receptive of your presence here, despite the peace it signifies."

My mind trips—because at this point in the book, when Kilian announces the peace ball, his men come around. They aren't waving Dawn Queen banners in the streets, but they begrudgingly admit that the union is a good idea.

I think back to Broderick's disdain for me when he brought me to Kilian's room. Was that *too* hate-filled? He should've been just a tad supportive at that point, right?

Something's missing. Something happened in the book that didn't happen here to—

My eyes go wide. Round, saucer-like, and I bat my eyelashes to hide the sudden flush of adrenaline that surges through my veins.

Kilian doesn't miss it, tracking my every move. "Sloane darling—what troubles you?"

I stare at the rumbled bedding, gathering my resolve.

Can I say this?

Can I…*ask* for this?

Do I *want* this?

Because I know what's missing. I know what scene *didn't* happen that *should have* happened, because it broke down the barriers around Kilian's men and gave them the satisfaction of seeing their enemy brought low, conquered by Kilian utterly. They celebrate the union of Isaura and their High Prince because for them it is built on Kilian's domination.

They support Kilian and the Dawn Queen because they watched Isaura fuck his brains out on the High Prince's throne.

My cheeks go scalding hot and Kilian touches me there, his fingertips cool. "Sloane? What are you thinking?"

That scene in the book is one of the hottest moments in the entire series.

I've reread it countless times.

I've gotten myself off to it countless times.

To live it. To know half a dozen incredibly sexy men are watching me have sex, riled between hatred and arousal while their master uses my body for his pleasure…

This isn't real. It's just for fun.

But I know that's been a lie from the beginning.

This is my fantasy. I'm in control.

How often does a girl get this opportunity?

I turn to Kilian, eyes still wide, but doe-like, innocent—and a little scared. Isaura didn't have to talk Kilian into this in the book, and my mouth goes dry now.

How do you ask your hot fae boyfriend to fuck you in front of his guards?

"I think I know how to convince your men that this union is to be trusted." My words are whisper-quiet—but hot. Aching.

Kilian's face flashes with confusion before he notes my tone. "How so?"

I trace a line down his neck, to his collarbone, his chest, down, down, all the way to the tip of his cock.

"I'm willing to prove to them that the Dawn Queen has conceded to you," I tell him, breasts pressing together. My look up at him is as intensely sexy as I can make it, my wide eyes, my tongue darting out to wet my swollen lips. "In every way."

CHAPTER 11: KILIAN

I sit on this bed, a gorgeous, naked woman in my arms, and I cannot make sense of what she offers.

My cock does. It goes rock-hard, and her dainty fingers take advantage of it, stroking the shaft in gentle, sure pulses.

"Sloane," I manage her name. "You are offering to let my men see me with you."

"I am," she says with no hesitation, no shame, no awkwardness.

It is a sign of her trust in me. It is a sign of her faith in our union.

I can feel a spot of precum leak from my tip. Sloane swirls her thumb in it and glides her hand back along my shaft, and I have to close my eyes to keep from flinging her back and claiming her again. My wings arch high, ready to send me lurching towards her.

A war brews in my chest.

Desire to keep her all mine.

Desire to have my men on our side.

It will work. She has guessed the needs of my soldiers more effectively than even I would have. They reveled in seeing her bound in my dungeon; how much more would they enjoy seeing me take her, her body shuddering at my touch, my name screaming from her lips?

I rock towards her, thrusting into her hand, and I let the need take me to push her flat on her back. My wings pump the air once, billowing her hair back from her face, and I hear her go breathless in the gust.

"I agree to this," I say into her cheek, my hand on her throat, pinning her to the blankets. "But on my terms."

"Name them." Her voice is all need.

"The first—they will not touch you. I share with no one. They will watch only."

"Hmm," she agrees. I'm rocking against her, my hard cock spearing her thigh, unsatisfied, seeking.

"The second—they are allowed to speak. In fact, I insist on hearing what they think of the things I do to you."

Her lips part, a soundless agreement as I kiss my way across her shoulder, lips trailing over the heaving mound of one perfect breast.

"The third." I pause to flick my tongue on her nipple, the hardened bud stiffening more, and Sloane whimpers, pressing deeper into the blankets. "You will speak as well. You will tell them how good it feels, the things I do to you. You will tell them exactly who is commanding your body to come."

"All right," Sloane croons. "All right. I will—"

I suck her nipple into my mouth, teeth grazing the tip, and she moans in the core of her chest.

"I have one more," I say, kissing my way down her stomach. "The fourth—I am selfish. And I have many men in my guard. I do not want them all watching you. So you will decide how many we will let into the room."

That makes her eyes focus on me. "How-how many? I—"

"You will decide how many," I drop to my knees at the foot of the bed and spread her legs wide, showing me the folds of her perfect cunt in the firelight, "by how long it takes you to come in my mouth."

"Kilian—I—"

"For every second it takes you to come, one of my guards will be allowed to watch me fuck you." I peek up to see her wide eyes gazing back at me.

She doesn't protest. She doesn't argue.

Her chest rises and falls in quick, stunted breaths.

I grin as I bend down to her sweet cunt. "The count starts now," I purr and flick her with my tongue. "One."

CHAPTER 12: SLOANE

My body is still in that state of overstimulation where every touch feels like lightning—so it shouldn't take me long to come, especially with Kilian's mouth on my pussy.

He's torturous, though. He licks along my folds and declares, cruelly, "Two."

My back arches and I squirm against him as he drives his tongue into me, sweeping against my G-spot, not deep enough, not *enough*.

"Three."

"Kilian—please—"

"Yes, my lady—beg for me, just like that, when they watch."

Oh, fuck, fuck me—

"Four."

He licks my clit now with a fervor. He doesn't want many people to watch us—he's more selfish in that regard than I am.

I could tease him by holding out my orgasm intentionally. How long could I last?

"Five." His bark of frustration tells me he wants me to come. He sucks my clit into his mouth and I mewl with my own frustration.

An orgasm is right on the edge—right

there—

I grind my teeth, willing it down with every fiber of my being.

"You are fighting me," Kilian states with the authority of someone who is not used to being challenged. His wings beat the air once, lurching him deeper into me, and I stifle a gasp.

"Oh," I feign innocence through my teasing smile, "I thought you wanted me to hold out? I can, you know—what are we at now? Eight seconds? Nine? And how many men are in your battalion?"

The growl he emits is predatory, dark, and matches the sudden glint of bloodlust in his eyes. "Come for me, Sloane. Now."

"Ten," I count, staring fixated on the canopy bed.

I won't think about his tongue flicking my clit.

I won't think about the sensitivity building, building—

"Sloane. I said *come*," he demands, and then he *bites*, teeth barely sinking into that tender bud until it shatters in his mouth.

I scream, body thrashing, but Kilian plants his arms over me and pins me down, forcing me to feel every ounce of this pleasure I tried to deny myself. And he draws it out too, mouth and teeth staying firmly in place, even as the orgasm turns to sensitivity and my screams fade to whimpers.

Kilian climbs up my body and grabs a handful of my hair in his fist to make me look at him. His wings peel back so the firelight shines on my face, highlighting him too, the severity in his tense jaw. "You will not show disobedience when they watch."

It's a plea more than a command.

I kiss him. His lips are wet with my juices, the taste of me in his mouth sending me reeling even more.

"I won't," I promise. "I'll be your obedient Dawn Queen."

"Mine," he echoes and pushes his hips against me, letting me feel the hardness of his cock on my thigh.

My legs are already spread for him, my pussy wet and ready—I thrust up, but he pulls back with a smirk.

"Ah, my lady." He drags his hand down my stomach. "Not yet."

"Not—" I prop up on my elbows.

Oh shit.

He wants to do this *now*.

A spark of fear clashes with the desperate surge of need that has me leaving my legs splayed.

Maybe it's the blush staining my chest. Maybe it's the way I suddenly can't get my breathing to slow.

Whatever it is, Kilian bends back over me

and kisses me, long and deep, until my body relaxes into the bedding.

"You are mine, Sloane," he tells me. "I mean that. And I protect what is mine. You will be safe, and if at any point it is too much, simply say *dawn*, and it will end."

A safe word.

I'm doing something that requires needing a *safe word*.

A giggle bubbles through me and I dig the heels of my palms into my eyes. "Okay. Okay. I'm okay."

"Yes, you are." Kilian moves off of me, and I think he leaves—

Until I feel a familiar cold, hard metal encircle my right wrist.

I look up and Kilian guides me to sit.

"Put your arms here," he instructs, and I obey, my brain in a white fog as he manacles me around the post of his bed.

He kisses me again, fingers tangling in my hair. "You are my fantasy come to life," he tells me. "And you will make them all writhe with wondering why they spent so long hating you when they could have pleasured themselves to your image instead."

I nip at his lower lip. "That doesn't make you jealous, High Prince? That they will return to the barracks and jerk themselves off to the memory of your cock in me?"

Kilian pulls away and slowly begins dressing. Black pants, a tight silk shirt. With every move, his eyes stay on mine.

"Oh, they won't think about my cock when your body hangs here on display," but there's a twist in his voice. He *is* jealous, and it's that jealousy that I know will keep me safe, that will make this even hotter, even more unhinged.

Kilian hesitates, banter settling, and when he kisses me again, it's softer, sweeter. "I love you," he says into my forehead, a final, parting kiss, before he slips out the door.

And I'm left, chained to his bed, waiting for Kilian Kilnmor to return with his guards so they can watch him fuck the Dawn Queen.

I can only bend my forehead to the canopy post and laugh. It doesn't really help the growing bubble of nerves, but I giggle helplessly, body shivering even though the room is almost uncomfortably warm.

Then the door groans open.

CHAPTER 13: KILIAN

Five of my guards follow me willingly.

Sloane made it to ten seconds, but that was only after she defied me by resisting.

So she will have five watching her.

My jealousy only extends so far.

The closest in my circle follow me from the barracks, back up to my chambers. They do not know what I have planned, merely that I selected them by name and bid them come. Broderick is with them, and four others, childhood friends—Micah was nowhere to be found, but all the better. He is not a leader among the men, not the way Broderick and the other four are. If their minds are swayed, the rest will follow.

I stop before the closed door to my chambers. A tremor creeps up my limbs—not nerves, but eagerness.

Eagerness for all the times the Dawn Queen's armies left ours in tattered heaps.

Eagerness for all the times the Dawn Queen's strategy outplayed my own.

Eagerness, and vengeance, and penance, all things crashing and rising through me, so when I turn to face my men, I am wicked in the dim morning light of the hall.

"Gentlemen," I say to them. "Honored soldiers of Precipice. You have by now heard of the upcoming celebration in honor of my peaceful union with the Dawn Queen."

Broderick's jaw clenches. The others look away.

"Your disdain has been noted," I continue. "And it comes not without cause. But this morning, in the hours of the dawn itself, you will be given reason to believe not merely this peace, but that the Dawn Queen herself has submitted to me, and beseeches you all to know that she will pay fealty for her parts in the war."

"Fealty?" Broderick huffs a laugh. "She is far too proud for that. You may think her submissive to you, but we fear, High Prince, that that is part of her ploy to—"

I open the door behind me.

It swings wide, and there she is, handcuffed to the bed post. She turns to face the door, the tips of her cheekbones scarlet, her hair tumbling in untamed waves down to her midback.

She doesn't fight her restraints—no, those are for show more than purpose, to let the men see that she *chose* to be chained, as well as to show them that she has none of her magic in this. She chose all of this, and as such is willingly mine.

I enter first and stand aside. When the men

stay rigid in the hall, shocked mostly, I wave them in, impatient.

My cock is hard still—if I am not inside her warm cunt soon, that arousal will twist to aggression. Already I was forced to find no release as she broke apart under my mouth; I am aching for her, aching for all of this.

That need enhances with every step my men take into the room. Their eyes stay engrossed on her—only Broderick cuts a look at me.

"Sir?" His voice is dry. He swallows, furrowed brows darkening his shock.

"She has agreed to this," I tell them and shut the door after them. The bolt turns. "She submits to me in every way. This war has taken much from us—but it gives as well."

I cross the room, too aware of my tight pants restraining my cock.

The men form a half circle a few paces back from the bed, the tension emanating off of them so tangible it tastes of sweat and iron on the air.

Sloane eyes each of them, her blush deepening. Does she try to twist away, to shield her body from their sight? Shyness will not do, not on the face of the Dawn Queen.

I put two fingers under her chin and press my lips to her ear. "Remember who you are, my lady."

She leans back into me, her eyes flickering

shut as she bends her neck to lock my lips with hers. The kiss works her throat; I feel the muscles contracting there, and I trail my fingers down her neck to take one breast in my hand and squeeze.

"Shit," one of the men gasps.

"Are you all right?" I whisper to her.

Her nod comes quick and desperate, her eyes still closed. "Yes. Yes, please."

My lips quirk. "So eager."

Our voices had been low, but at that, Sloane's eyes spring open, and she grins.

"Yes, my lord," she says, louder. "Please. Please fuck me, sir."

I play with her nipple, stretching it, pinching it, rolling it between my fingers. Each move has her trembling, waves that ripple through me where my clothed form is fitted against hers.

There is absolute silence from the men. I spare a glance to see them utterly motionless, their cocks straining against their pants, the looks in their eyes flickering from painful arousal to satisfaction as their wings pulse and twitch behind them. Even Broderick, whose hatred of Sloane burns strongest; his eyes are riveted to the spot where my fingers pull at her nipple.

"What should I do with one who begs so sweetly?" I ask them.

Broderick's eyes don't leave her body. "Fuck her." After a beat, he adds, "High Prince."

The men grunt their agreement, some strained.

I sweep the hair over Sloane's shoulder. Desperation makes her bump her round ass back against me.

I catch her hips, hold them firmly in place.

I should draw it out.

Make them frenzied for it.

Make *her* delirious for it.

But my need is a living, writhing creature, and I will go feral if I am not within her, *now*.

I undo the ties on my pants to pull out my cock. Without pretense, I part her cheeks, angle her cunt to me, and slam into her.

Sloane throws her head back with a guttural cry. "My prince—is too—too big—"

This is the first time I have taken her in this position, and I realize for a moment that perhaps I *am* too large for this angle—but she shifts her hips back, taking me deeper, and the noise she makes—

The sheer, delicious *cry*—

I arch over her, teeth sinking into her shoulder. The chains of her manacles rattle as she grips the post, hands white-knuckled around the wood.

"Who is fucking you?" I growl into her ear. My wings spread, not their full width, but enough to cut a harsh image around me. Their shadow casts over her, painting her in gray darkness.

"The Night Prince," she whimpers. "You, sir—the Night Prince——"

It ends in a strangled gasp as I pull back and slam into her once, twice, then rapidly, pumping hard and fast into her tight, warm cunt. But it isn't enough, even these shuddering noises she's making——

I reach around, hands delving into her soft folds, and find her clit.

"Sir—yes, please—make me come—make me——" Her manacles rattle where she strains to reach down, but she cannot touch herself.

"Should I?" I ask it of the men. They are delirious now, sweating and tense—not a one reaches for their swollen dicks, though, and I commend them for their restraint.

"Only if she asks nicely," says Broderick, and I give a savage grin.

"You hear that, Sloane darling?" I stop rubbing her clit, but I reach up to continue the torment on her nipple, all the while pumping rapidly into her slick cunt. "How nicely can you ask for it?"

"Please, sir," she begs, begs harder than I thought her capable of, "please let me——"

"Oh, it isn't me you must ask," I growl into her ear. My fingers clamp around her nipple, pinching hard, and she mewls, head dropping back, sweat slicking down her heated skin.

Her gaze flicks to the men. Is this the first time she has looked at them since I entered her? It makes my cock twitch, all too ready to explode— that in this room full of eager men, she truly only has eyes for me.

Sex-crazed and dizzied, Sloane looks at each warrior in turn. That single look will do more to get them off than anything else we do—her eyes are wild with need and innocence, her hair in curled tangles that brush the tops of her breasts, her swollen lips catching once between her teeth.

"Please, sirs," she manages. "Please, can I come?"

There's a pause. I think they may deny her—

—but then Broderick nods. Once. Quick and fleeting.

I put my hand back on her clit and move my fingers in steady circles that match my slowed thrusts. Her whole body begins to shudder, and I feel the moment her orgasm takes her—her pussy clenches my cock so tightly that I have no choice but to follow her over the edge.

"Kilian!" she screams, body rippling with a visceral orgasm that shows every winding of muscle, every flicker of pleasure. "*Kilian—*"

The way she is twisted, her body angled towards the men, I wonder if she knows how enthralled she has all of us. They stare, slack jawed and entranced—of their own volition, as the manacles dampen any magic. Her shoulders peel back, her jaw setting. She must feel the power she exudes. We are hers, mere mortals left to grovel at her feet beneath the radiant glory of this creature in ecstasy.

I grunt through my own orgasm, holding back how inexplicably wondrous it is to be aligned with her, how beyond fucking this sensation has become.

My cock softens in her walls, and I cup my arm around her stomach, the other propped just over her hands on the post. My forehead rests between her shoulder blades as I drag in breaths, trying to level myself.

"You are dismissed," I tell the men without looking at them.

There's a moments pause. Then feet shuffle; the door unlocks, opens, closes again.

We are alone.

I undo her manacles, and I am ready when Sloane falls limp; I catch her easily, scooping her into my arms, kissing her cheeks, her hair, her lips.

"You did beautifully, my lady," I say to her.

She looks up at me, exhausted and satisfied, and when she smiles, I am enthralled anew.

CHAPTER 14: SLOANE

I have the days off work until my next session at Club Reverie, so I haul up in my apartment and pour over my copies of *Night Prince and Dawn Queen.*

In between reliving what was the single hottest moment of my entire life. But no matter how many times I got off to thoughts of *Night Prince and Dawn Queen* before, now, it feels…less than. Faded. The real thing was so crystalline and visceral that even the memory of it isn't enough to sustain me.

I want more. I want back in. I want Kilian, want him so badly that I have to resist begging Devyn to let me have an extra session every week.

No. *No.* I will not lose my access. I will be controlled.

So, instead of focusing on the expert way Kilian uses my body—because, honestly, *what the fuck*—I pour myself into research.

I pull open my laptop and scour the fan boards.

I even drag out my massive, illustrated copy of *The World of Precipice* until every free space in my tiny living room is covered in some variation of this series.

Isaura didn't know that the archmage who cursed her was part of Kilian's court. She approached him for the power to defeat the High Prince of Fort Precipice when she was at Ambrose's court—right before her mother revealed the true reason for Isaura's visit there: that she was a warprize for Ambrose, his bride-to-be. But Isaura had already made the deal with the archmage for the power to kill the *Night Prince*, not just *any* enemy; and so Ambrose quickly subdued her magic with his own tricks.

Then Isaura found herself even more trapped when her savior turned out to be the Night Prince himself.

And she fell in love with him.

She thought if she could find that archmage, she could get him to undo their deal—but when the archmage revealed himself, he was much closer than she'd anticipated.

He was Micah, Kilian's brother.

But he was not truly Micah at all; he had killed the real Micah while Kilian and his entourage were in Ambrose's court, just after Isaura made her deal with him. The archmage took Micah's face and slipped into the Precipice court, slowly weakening it here, there. Archmages run amok in the world of *Night Prince and Dawn Queen*—there's a ton of fan speculation that they aren't simple mages at all, but gods in disguise, and that all of the machinations and messes they make are building up to a larger war between gods that the author will reveal in the final books of the series.

But what I'm focused on now is simpler than that.

I want to know what will happen if I tell Kilian about Micah now.

In the book, the confrontation with Micah doesn't happen for a while; they have the ball, then Kilian and Isaura travel around a bit, solidifying their union, building peace. They even run into Ambrose again, but he's powerless against the might of the unified Night Prince and Dawn Queen, and he sulks like the shriveled little toddler he is. Through the course of their travels, Isaura's curse grows; and when she can't fight it any longer, she tries to leave.

Only Kilian doesn't let her. Obviously.

And Micah is there to make sure she stays too. He *wants* Kilian dead, for the chaos it will create. Isaura tries to kill Kilian, then runs. But since she failed, Micah forces her to return; and when that confrontation unfolds, together, Kilian and Isaura kill the fake-Micah.

But in the story I'm living at Club Reverie, I don't have Isaura's curse. Devyn did say it isn't an *exact* replica of this story and world—maybe Micah isn't even an archmage in disguise?

I ask Devyn exactly that before my next session.

She grins at me over the tablet. "Why should I tell you? Seems an unfair advantage if you want accuracy."

"Oh yeah, I won't enjoy it at all if you spoil the ending for me."

She rolls her eyes. "I'll tell you if you answer some questions for me first. Standard debrief."

But she looks away, focused on the screen a bit too intently.

"Sure," I say and shift in the chair.

The first half dozen questions are pretty standard—any physical side effects that linger? Any headaches, any blurred vision, any stiffness or muscle issues?

Then Devyn pauses. "In your fantasy sessions, how would rate Kilian's actions towards you?"

I flinch. "What do you mean?"

"I mean—does he seem accurate wholly to the character you expect, or does he respond and adapt to the changes you have made to the narrative?"

I think back on my conversations with him. The way I could see something shifting behind Kilian's eyes, like he could tell when I went off-book.

"He responds and adapts." I smile, but it softens. "It's pretty amazing, actually. Makes it even easier to forget it isn't real."

Devyn types something into the tablet. Her eyes cut up to me. "Who says it isn't real?"

I wait for the punchline. For her to laugh.

When silence stretches, I chuckle. "Um. You did? All that promo about fantasies and shit?"

"Our brains cannot tell the difference between certain imagined sensations and reality. What I mean is—" Devyn bites her lips together. After another long pause, she bats her hand. "Never mind me. I wax poetic sometimes—and over what is in essence just a computer program." But she winces, and I can tell; to her, it's anything but *just a computer program.*

I shift towards her. "You seem like you're trying to tell me something. Like, a lot. Did I do something wrong?"

"No! No. Really, you can ask Naz—I get off in my own world sometimes. Part of why I made Club Reverie, actually."

"Naz?"

She shrugs toward the door. "Oh—my husband. He ducked in last time?"

Her cheeks are stained pink.

There's still something she's trying not to say, something she wants desperately to say, but she pushes the button for the headset, and it starts to lower.

"Oh! One more thing—" Devyn spins to face me and my heart catches in my throat.

But she just grins. "Micah is an archmage. You don't have Isaura's curse in this storyline because most who choose this fantasy opt not to have the desire to murder Kilian clogging up their enjoyment. I can add it in if you like?"

Her finger hovers over the tablet.

"No!" I chirp. "I'm...I'm good. Thanks— yeah, it is better."

She smiles. "Then relax and have fun."

She could add Isaura's curse to my storyline with the push of a button.

This isn't real. It's just for fun.

But Devyn seemed physically opposed to that mindset.

Who says it isn't real?

I shake my head, fighting to clear the questions, the probing, the weird, lingering itch that being around Devyn leaves in my head anymore. The things she's insinuating with her questions, her whole demeanor—

Does she think these fantasies *are* real somehow?

But before I can really linger on that, I open my eyes, and I'm in Fort Precipice's throne room.

It's starkly different from the first time I

stood here, confronting Kilian in a gown dripping sexuality. Though, honestly, the gown I'm wearing now isn't much different—gold again, the color of the Dawn Queen, only this time the fabric grips my neck tightly before hugging every curve down to my ankles, where it flares out behind me in a rippling waterfall of glitter.

The throne room reflects that gold color, only wrapped in black, a show of unity between the Night Prince and the Dawn Queen. Banners and accents, cloths covering tables piled with food, candelabras and chandeliers dripping obsidian and gold—the room is a perfect marriage of our two nations.

It's a perfect marriage of *us*.

My heart catches in my throat as Kilian steps out from behind me.

"You like it?" he asks with a sparkle in his eye that makes him look younger, eager, and I remember from the book—he designed this event himself, oversaw the decorations and the styling, all to make Isaura happy.

I nod, grinning. "It's perfect, Kilian. Really."

He takes my hands and nods over my shoulder. Behind me, a door groans open.

"Then let it begin," he says, but his eyes are on me as guests begin to file in.

The pause as they enter lets me truly see

Kilian. He's cleaned up as strikingly as the room. His black suit is lined with gold that glitters as he moves, and his hair is swept back in its usual high poof, only when he tips his head, the candlelight catches—is that gold glitter swirling across his skin?

I laugh and press closer to him, smelling the heady spice of him, and when he bends his lips to mine, it is the most fitting image for guests to see: our union made real.

Music kicks up. Joviality permeates the air—Kilian's men did quick work towards getting the guard on our side, and they are the first to begin dancing, stoking the room to embrace our allegiance.

Kilian guides me through the room, greeting guests, smiling at those who have come. I recognize some people from the Dawn Queen's court, regaled in draping gold robes, and they bow when we approach.

It is such a wild, wonderful sensation, being on Kilian's arm, wearing a dress more gorgeous than anything I've ever been in. And the fact that it's still my body, not an approximation of Isaura— that it's been *my body* doing all of this, actually—is what infuses me to stand tall, to be the queen I am. None of this has been playacting a role. It's just been *me*, and here I am now, grinning helplessly every time I catch Kilian gazing at me.

We reach the end of the room and steal a moment off to the side, watching the dancers spin. Only because I'm pressed against him, as close as is appropriate in a room full of courtiers, I feel Kilian take a sharp breath.

"He doesn't dance," Kilian whispers, and when I follow his eyes, I see Micah.

Leaning against the wall.

Watching us.

Watching *me*.

My throat swells. I try to focus back on the dancers, on the glitz and glitter of this miraculous evening; but my brain keeps circling back to Micah. To this lingering threat that I could undo, just like that, and all Kilian and I would have to worry about going forward would be how many hours we could reasonably spend in his bed.

I look up at him, and Kilian nuzzles my cheek.

It will crush him. It does when it happens in the book; but if I tell him now, if he can confront Micah knowing that that is *not* his brother...

I twist to fold myself into Kilian's arms. "Can we speak somewhere?"

Kilian's grin turns heated. "Speak? Mm." He bites at my ear. "My thoughts exactly."

Oh, fuck me—maybe we shouldn't speak in private. Because my pussy is already wet at the thought of letting him take me in some dark closet…

"No," I say, arching up to put my lips to his ear. "Later. I really need to tell you something."

His hands clamp to my spine. A severity falls over him when he pulls back. "All right. This way."

We slip out a side door—of course people notice; but we wave them off, and they likely assume we're sneaking off to fuck too.

By the time Kilian leads me into a meeting room, a long table spread with maps of Precipice, I tell myself maybe I should just seduce him. I can tell him later about Micah. Or not at all—who knows how Micah's involvement will play out now that I didn't make any sort of deal with him?

But he's still a traitor in Kilian's court. He still murdered Kilian's brother to get here.

Kilian sits on the table and takes my hands, pulling me between his spread legs. "What does my lady have to tell me?"

I clear my throat. Nerves make my hands shake, and he squeezes them, firm but caring. That change in my demeanor shifts him too, curious to alert.

"What's wrong?" he asks. Demands. There is the High Prince.

"Kilian—I—" Fuck. How do I even say this? "Remember when I gave you that list of spies and traitors?"

His lips flash in a grin. "Vividly."

My cheeks heat. "Not *that*. Well—no, not that, not now. There's one name I should have added. One name I think you'll want to hear."

Kilian's brow furrows. He stays silent.

"Micah. Micah Kilnmor."

Hardness settles over his face. "What do you mean?"

"He isn't your brother. He's an archmage who killed Micah while you were in Ambrose's court. He means to sow discord in your kingdom—and he means to kill you."

Kilian flinches, drawing me closer. After a long moment of his eyes darting through mine, his lips part.

"How do you know this?"

Oh, fuck. What would make the most sense in this world, in this storyline?

"I—I saw him. While I was in Ambrose's court. I knew him as an archmage with a different face, but now—" Fuckity fuck fuck, how do I explain that I know the archmage is Micah? What, did I *see* him murder and then take on the Kilnmor brother's body? Shit. I didn't think this through.

Kilian seems to be piecing together the holes in my story just as I am.

His grip on my hands goes from caring to painfully tight. "There is something you are not telling me, Dawn Queen."

I fight to keep from ripping out of his grip.

I fight to keep from blubbering.

That look in his eyes—it's the hardness he always showed to Isaura, in the book. The distance he kept carefully between them until the very end. But *I* bridged that distance immediately; *me*, Sloane, the relationship we have now, open and honest and true—

Only it isn't.

It never has been.

Tears prick my eyes.

Fuck. What do I have to lose?

Everything, everything, everything—

"I know this about Micah," I say, mouth dry, voice soft, "because I'm not from this world."

The crease between Kilian's brows deepens.

"I came here thanks to…to magic. In my world, you—this—Precipice, the war, the Dawn Queen—it's all a story. So I know about Micah, and how he isn't really Micah, because I've read your story. I've read your story so many times, Kilian."

This is absolutely crazy.

What the *fuck* have I done.

But I've said it, and it hangs there, and I hold my breath as I watch Kilian's face.

Maybe I can reset. Maybe I can have Devyn undo this, go back to before I told Kilian any of this—

His grip on my hands drops. Entirely.

He lets me go and stands up.

I back away, letting him pace, his hands at the small of his back.

"My brother is dead?" he asks, his back to me.

"Yes," I say, stupidly.

He paces.

Again, he pauses. "What else should I know of the future? Battles to come, defeats looming, enemies—" he doesn't look at me, but his words twist "—who will be my undoing?"

"Just Micah. Or, the not-Micah. Many of the kingdoms who pose as your enemies are tired of war, same as you. They're only spurred to it because of archmages like the one who killed your brother."

He nods sharply. Paces again.

"Kilian," the way I say his name is a desperate beg. "Kilian—look at me, please."

"So where you come from," his eyes stay heavy on the floor, "I am a work of fiction?"

"You're real to me."

He shakes his head on a huff of brittle laughter. "And you spend how much time here? Days? Hours?"

"Hours at a time. I—it's difficult to explain."

"What do you do when you are not with me?"

Now he does look at me, and I feel like my whole world is unraveling.

"I—" What do I do when I'm not here?

I work at a shitty coffee shop.

I go back to my tiny, empty apartment.

I'm rude to my only sort of friend.

"Nothing," I say, and it kicks out of me with a sob.

Kilian doesn't rush to me. The fact that I expect him to breaks me more.

"All you do is visit this place through magic, and nothing more?" He asks it not condescendingly, but sadly. "I find that hard to believe, that one such as you would find solace in so narrow a purpose. You are—" He blinks quickly, realization dawning that he does not truly know how to finish that sentence. Who am I, really?

"I'm Sloane," I tell him quickly. "I'm not— I'm not the Dawn Queen. But my name really is Sloane. And I—" I hesitate, the weight of how pathetic I am nearly crushing me. "Being here has made me feel more alive than any moment in my own reality. You make me stronger out there, Kilian. Because of what we do in here. And everything I feel for you is real."

Kilian's eyes are bloodshot. His jaw is set. I

am wholly unable to read the emotion on his face, sorrow or disgust or anger.

"I will investigate these allegations against Micah," he tells me, his voice stone cold and even.

I nod. "Of course. How can I help?"

Kilian frowns at me. "Help?"

Something seizes in my chest. The feeling of a cliff coming, an edge I can't see, and I'm stumbling blindly in the dark.

"Yes. I—does this change things?"

Idiot.

Of course this changes things.

Kilian turns away, his gaze fixed on the wall opposite him. "You need to leave, Sloane."

"Kilian," his name comes on a gust of air, his words slamming into my stomach.

"You need to leave," he says again. "I cannot pretend to understand what magics you speak of, but I know—anything that powerful cannot be used frivolously."

"Frivolously? I didn't—" But my words die. This is frivolous.

This isn't real. It's just for fun.

I shake my head, tears tumbling down my cheeks. "Please, Kilian, just let me explain this better. I didn't—I can't leave you. I can't leave this."

I grab his arm.

Touching him centers me. It changes him,

too, his lips parting on a sip of breath, his eyes rolling shut.

"You say a powerful archmage has taken my brother's form," he says, his eyes still shut. "And you say a powerful magic is the reason for your existence here at all."

"Kilian," but I can't think of anything else to add, any explanation that will fix the realization he's coming to.

"Magic such as this is addictive," he continues. "It is corruptive. And I cannot let it corrupt you, Sloane."

"No, please——"

"You need to leave. Now."

"Kilian——"

He shrugs off my hand and turns for the door.

"Kilian!" I sob his name, but he doesn't stop.

He doesn't look back.

The High Prince of Fort Precipice walks out of the room, leaving me broken in his wake, and he doesn't spare me a parting glance.

"Sloane! Sloane, breathe!"

A hand pats my cheek. I blink at bright lights flashing, and somewhere, someone sighs in relief.

"She's back. Sloane, can you hear us?"

Us?

Not Kilian.

I feel Club Reverie's chair under me. The helmet being slowly pulled off my head.

"Your vitals started to go haywire—what happened in there? Are you all right?" Devyn holds my hand, her body bent over mine to look down into my eyes.

Next to her, reading the results on a blood pressure cuff attached to my arm, is her husband, Naz.

Devyn pulls my focus back. "Sloane—you need to tell me what happened. Did something glitch? Did you—"

Tears fall. I cup my hands over my face and sob, heaving wretches that rock me into a ball on the chair.

Devyn's hands go to my shoulders. She shares a look with Naz who obediently slips out of the room.

"Sloane." Her voice is softer, gentler. "What happened?"

"How—how was he allowed to do that?" I'm too broken to be angry, but I suddenly think I *should* be angry at her. It's her stupid fantasy creator, her fucked-up programing.

"Do what, Slo—"

"He *broke up with me*. How could he even do that? What the fuck, Devyn—" I sob anew, because saying it out loud is so fucking pathetic; and because everything in me is absolutely shredded.

The look on Kilian's face.

The betrayal.

The heartache.

And now he's left to pick up the pieces without me——

Only he won't. Because as long as I'm not in the program, he doesn't exist. Right?

"I need to leave." I shove Devyn off and stand. "I need to go home."

"Sloane, please—let's talk about——"

"Fuck off!" I scream it at her. She backs up, hands lifted, but her face is a tangled mess of sorrow and...

Curiosity?

Fuck her curiosity, really, *I can't handle this*.

"Just—just leave me alone," I whimper, and I push out the door, past Naz in the hall, through the front lobby, and out into my drizzly, cold reality.

A drizzly, cold reality that I was just *fine* with until Devyn came and offered everything I ever wanted, everything I could have had a totally okay, mundane existence without.

And now?

Now, I know exactly how my fantasy would play out.

I know exactly how my wild wishes would end up.

In heartbreak.

CHAPTER 15: KILIAN

As long as I live, I will never forgive myself for putting that look on Sloane's face.

But all of what she said—it is too powerful. She plays with fates she does not understand, and I—

I cannot risk it. Not for Precipice. Not for her.

I cannot risk it, I tell myself, hard, as I stalk back to the party.

Our party.

I do not know if she obeyed me, but she does not follow; she must have left. Used her too-powerful magic to slip back to her reality.

Her reality where I do not exist.

Her reality where she does, as she said, *nothing*. Could her world truly be empty but for this?

I stop, one hand to my chest, the other braced against the cold stone wall in this empty hall.

If I do not exist where she comes from—

—does she exist here?

And if I am fictional in her world, how am I here still, beyond her sight, beyond her influence?

Would I not cease to exist apart from her?

Threads are fraying. My mind spins, heaves—and I still have Micah to deal with.

Micah, who has not been the same since our time at Ambrose's court.

What she says aligns with my suspicions, but I will investigate. I will have Broderick and my other trusted men figure out a way to ensnare Micah—or whoever he is—so we may test the validity of these claims.

My head throbs, an ache bouncing down the back of my neck.

How I tire of this.

Constant war.

Endless lies.

Would that Sloane had taken me with her.

The thought spears through my chest.

I want to rage at someone—anyone—I want to wail my frustration at *something*. Because I sent away the love of my life, and I do not know what to do now. Because I am alone, again; fighting wars and dodging threats, *again*, and all I want is to sweep her into my arms and undo the last moments, to pretend we are simply *us*.

Music plays from the throne room. Our party continues.

What does Sloane's disappearance mean for our alliance? Without the Dawn Queen, her armies will be leaderless; easy enough to sway them to our side against a common enemy. Maybe this archmage, even.

Exhaustion makes my chest ache.

I scrub at my eyes, scraping down to the last flickers of my resolve to drudge up the stoic image I must carry now.

I look up, shoulders level as I walk back towards the throne room—and a figure emerges from the darkness ahead of me.

Not one of the guests, not even a courtier of the Dawn Queen by their dress. I do not recognize this person.

And they are in my fort.

My wings flare out and I rip twin daggers from hidden sheaths at my thighs. "Name yourself."

The figure takes a step forward until their—her—face is lit by the flickers of a lit wall sconce behind me. "We need to talk."

CHAPTER 16: SLOANE

I sit in my apartment.

My empty, shitty apartment.

I eat. Maybe. There's some leftovers in my fridge. I sleep—probably too much, bundled in a thick hoodie and smothered under blankets until the crushing weight in my chest is matched by the weight on my body.

When I wake up one time, my eyes focus on the stack of books on my nightstand. *Fort of Night and Edge* is right on top.

A gasp bursts out of me.

For years, those books were my safe space. My escape. My anchor.

Looking at them now, all I feel is pain.

Pain, and…emptiness.

I really only had this one thing in my life. This one obsession that permeated every area of my existence.

And now? Who am I without it?

I've relived the conversation with Kilian so many times. Every time, it kills me all over again, how I had no good answers to his simplest of questions.

"What do you do when you are not with me?"

"Nothing."

I sit up in my bed, eyes fixed on those books.

"All you do is visit this place through magic, and nothing more?"

He'd been surprised. Shocked. Saddened. That all I was doing in this reality was escaping to his.

"I find that hard to believe, that one such as you would find solace in so narrow a purpose."

I throw off my blankets and kick open my closet.

Each book hits the wall inside it with a dull thunk. I throw the first book in the series—the third—the illustrated world guide—the fourth—I grab artwork off my walls, fanart I'd bought or printed, and I throw that so hard the glass frames shatter.

I snatch the last thing—*Fort of Night and Edge*. The second book.

Tears burning my eyes, I let it fly, heaving it across the room with all my strength, all my shame, all my sadness. My lips part and I cry out as it soars, smashing into the wall, the pages bending, the spine cracking.

I slam my closet door.

Forehead to the wood.

I breathe.

Jacked Up isn't open yet.

The moment I step inside, my whole body aches. I don't want to be here. Not in a *ugh I don't wanna work today* way, but in a deep, soul-wrenching, *this is not where I should be.*

Where *should* I be, then?

I've never asked myself that. I've only ever done the bare minimum so I could have my escape and fantasies. I never lingered too much on the real world because it was never a priority.

"Hey!" Eden pops out of the backroom with a bunch of empty cup stacks in her arms. She nods behind her and mouths *Kyle is in a MOOD.*

Normally, I'd nod back and thank her for the warning.

But now?

That rings in my head. Over and over.

What now?

Eden puts the cups down and stops, her eyes narrowing on me. "Hey, you okay? You look…"

I know exactly how I look. Gaunt and exhausted. Like I've just been broken up with.

Fuck. I hate even thinking that. *It wasn't real.* If I was in any mood to talk to her, I'd ask Devyn how many people have gotten her program to turn on them like I did. Maybe I hold some kind of record.

God, the depths of my pitifulness know no

bounds. And honestly, I'm fucking *tired* of feeling that way. I'm tired of feeling awkward and uncomfortable in my own skin. I'm just…

"I'm just really fucking tired," I say to Eden.

Before I can think why, I cross the room to the break area.

Inside, Kyle sits at the kitchen table, papers spread around him, grumbling to numbers.

He doesn't even look up. "Any drink slip ups today'll come directly out of your paycheck. I'm not fucking around anymore."

"Me neither. I quit."

Kyle whips his head up. "What did you say?"

"You heard me."

I turn around and walk right back out.

Eden is rigid at the counter, her eyes wide, a slow smile creeping across her face. "Did you just—"

I wince. "Yeah—fuck, that puts more on you, but I just—"

She waves her hand. "Are you kidding? You do you. Did you get another job or something?"

Kyle storms out of the backroom. He looks like he might say something, argue or yell at me, but I face him.

Not as Sloane.

Well…yes, as Sloane.

Fuck yes as Sloane.

Because the Sloane who was Isaura is still

this Sloane, and I am *here*, now, and so that's who I am as I face my asshole ex-boss.

A mother-fucking Dawn Queen.

Kyle actually lurches backwards when I look at him.

His mouth snaps shut and he ducks back into the room without a single fucking word, and oh my *god*, if that isn't the most satisfying thing I think I've ever accomplished.

Eden chirps a laugh before smacking her hands over her mouth. "I still have to work here. Shit. But," her voice lowers, "holy crap, Sloane, what's going on?"

"Honestly, I don't know yet," I say, and I smile. Like, *really* smile.

Because I just quit my shitty job and I have nothing lined up but—but this is *freedom*, isn't it? This is *possibility*.

I grin, keep right on grinning, as the front door chimes.

"We're not open yet!" Eden calls without even looking at them. "Well, good for you. Let me know where you end up—maybe I'll follow you to better pastures."

"I will," I say, and I mean that. I start to turn, but I stop and face her again. "Actually. You wanna hang out tonight? Grab dinner or something?"

Eden smiles, bright and wide. "Yeah. My

boyfriend's playing again. You can come."

"Sounds perfect." And it does. It really, truly does.

I turn, grinning still—

And run smack into the person who came in early.

They hadn't stepped back out at Eden's call. And when I blink up at them, I go rigid.

Devyn puts her hands up. "Before you say anything, I really must speak with you."

I start to pull back up that Dawn Queen Piss Off Look, but Devyn arches an eyebrow and bends closer to me.

"Please, Sloane," she says. "Five minutes of your time is all I ask. I promise, I will make it worth your while."

Well. As someone who very recently became unemployed...

"How worth my while?" I ask.

Devyn blinks quickly. "You're asking for money? Of course. Reimbursement for your sessions."

"Hm." I tap my heel on the floor. "Fine. Five minutes."

Club Reverie isn't open yet this early either. The receptionist isn't even in, but Devyn whisks us through the entryway. She hurries down the hall lined with the club rooms, nonfunctional right now, before opening the door to a room I haven't been in yet. Some kind of meeting area, or a break room maybe? A nice couch sits against one wall, a small table with chairs takes up the other side. There's a closed door near the back that Devyn eyes when we come in, but she turns to me so fast I barely have time to orient myself under the similarly low lighting and cozy, spa-like decorations before she takes my hands.

"Sloane," she says my name with a noticeable twist of joy, like she's fighting hard to keep from screeching happiness to the ceiling.

"This is a weird fucking mood for someone who let her program get so messed up," I cut back.

Devyn squeezes my hands. "I didn't write that program. What you experienced—it wasn't a program at all."

I pull my hands out of hers. "It was *real*, right? Why does it have to be fake? All that shit again. God, Devyn—I get it now, I really do. It wasn't real. None of it. So don't make it worse by—"

"That's what I'm trying to tell you." Devyn doesn't try to reach for my hands again, but she doesn't seem to know what to do with hers now that I've let go. She twists her fingers together, straightens her skintight beige dress, pats her hair. "Most—all of the rest, actually—of my clients at Club Reverie do enter a program I specifically created. We control every aspect of their environment and interactions so situations like your conversation with Kilian are an impossibility. They simply *do not* happen."

"So...I was some experiment?"

"No. Well, in a way, but not how you are thinking." Devyn pats her cheeks. "Oh my, how to explain this. Well, maybe a demonstration is better. How familiar are you with the *Wonder* series?"

"The superhero world? I've seen the movies, but it wasn't really my thing." I was too busy obsessing over *Night Prince and Dawn Queen*, but everyone and their mother has seen all the movies in the *Wonder* universe—dozens of different superheroes all fighting evil.

"Right. So you're familiar with the villain—Nazar?"

"Yeah? What does this have to do with anything?"

"Well—" She crosses to the closed door and ducks her head into whatever room is beyond. After a second, her husband comes out with her.

And my whole body goes numb.

Because not only is he attractive—which, duh, he's still insanely polished—I realize that I *recognize* him.

Nazar.

Not merely as the actor who played Nazar.

But some kind of living embodiment of that villain god who tormented various superheroes across seven movies and dozens of comic books.

Devyn takes his hand. "I spent years creating the most realistic virtual reality imaginable. I wanted to tap into every sense and create a full body experience. And I did. But—" She smiles up at him. "One trip in...something changed. I found I wasn't in the controlled world I had created, but a very close approximation to it. After a *lot* of research and unwinding what I had done, it turned out that I had ceased to be in my own program. This instance became less about virtual reality, and more a...a timeline bridge. A reality shift."

"A *what?*" I'm still staring, stricken, at Nazar.

One corner of his mouth lifts in something like a smile, which is honestly just way more terrifying.

"I don't bite," he says to me, but he flashes his teeth, and on some level that might've been sexy, but my brain is spinning like a mother fucking Ferris wheel.

"A reality shift," Devyn says. She tugs on Nazar's hand. "Love, please. She's going through enough."

He looks down at her. His expression changes—ferocious teasing to soft and tender.

"As I was saying," Devyn faces me, but her

body leans into Nazar, "I was able to shift into a reality where a version of Nazar was real. *This* version. And, through a rather delicate aligning of code, I was able to bring him to my timeline."

"Wait. Wait the fucking—*wait*." I'm too far from the couch to sit on it so I just sink to the floor, right here, in the middle of this weird spa-like break room. My knees press into the fluffy carpet, grounding me. "Oh my god. You're insane. This is insane, right? You're actually saying you *brought a man here from a different timeline*."

"Well," it's Nazar who speaks, and I have just enough control of my body to look up and see his mischievous, cruel smile, "two men now, actually."

"Two—"

"Darling, go get him," Devyn waves at Nazar. She crouches down in front of me and takes my hands again as he leaves. "Sloane, Club Reverie itself is fairly new, but I have been using this technology for years. I thought what happened with Nazar and myself was a glitch, but I've been trying to replicate it. And then…you came in. And I *knew*, I knew in a way I can't explain—I knew it would work for you, too."

I trip on something she said. "Go get—who? You mean I timeline jumped? Devyn, this is—"

Nazar returns.

But he isn't alone.

A shadow pulls out of the doorway behind him.

I thought my body had gone numb before. Now, I'm statue-still, and I'm glad I'm already kneeling on the floor, because the way my vision heaves, I know I'd fall over if I'd been standing.

Kilian.

Kilian, *here*.

"Hello, Sloane darling." He smiles at me, his focus only on me, just me. A heavy sense of relief pours off of him, and his hands clench and unclench at his sides.

I know that look.

He wants to hold me.

Even after—

I bend forward, face in my hands, shaking my head. "No. No, Devyn—this isn't *real*—I'm losing my fucking mind—"

Devyn's soft fingers loop my wrists and pull my hands down. The look in her eyes is utter resolution. Absolute certainty. The face of someone who has likely had to defend this very premise to whole boards of colleagues only to be met with disdain time and again.

"You began in the virtual simulation of Precipice, the same as many other clients," she says. "But it slowly began to shift. His reality overrode the program, until your time there really was *your time there*. It was why you never had any of

Isaura's powers or her curse—you were never playing her, you were *you*. And the times you were here took some finagling to fill in the gaps, but it allowed me to begin building the bridge to bring him to this timeline."

"You—you did *what* to him?" I look up at Kilian in horror.

"Willingly, Sloane!" Devyn waves her hands. "He came her willingly. He wanted to come here. To you."

CHAPTER 17: KILIAN

A tumult of events has taken my last days, but when I see her, I am centered.

My guard and I managed to capture and subdue the mage posing as Micah. He is bound now and powerless.

I sent word off to the other kingdoms, my allies and not, warning them of these archmages and the influence they hold over our perpetual state of war.

And in the midst of this, this woman, Devyn, explained more of what Sloane had tried to tell me. That she comes from a world not my own—and there was a way I could join her, if I wanted.

It was hardly a decision at all.

Every effort I undertook to subdue the archmage and solidify peace for my kingdom was not for my own future, but as a goodbye. Broderick will make as fine a High Prince as I ever did.

And now, I am here, in a world I do not understand—no magic, no *wings*, either, which is woeful to adapt to, but I will endure.

Because it means being here, with *her*.

I step forward. Nazar allows me to pass, but if he says something, I do not hear him; every part of me is fixated on the crumpled form of Sloane.

Devyn sees me approaching and rises, giving me her space.

Sloane gapes up at me. Tears streak her cheeks, her eyes wide and watery, and though I have known her only as the Dawn Queen, seeing her in her world for the first time I see all the best parts of her that I loved most. I see every emotion that brews in her written in the lines of her face.

"Kilian?" she gasps my name.

I kneel before her and hold out my hands. A brief moment of fear flashes through me—what if she does not want me here? What if I hurt her too badly with my insistence that she leaves?

"How can I make it up to you, my lady?" I ask of her.

"Make it up to me?" She squints, confusion taking her.

"How we parted. How I hurt you last we spoke. I did not understand the full breadth of this magic, and I—"

"*I* didn't understand it. I still don't, fuck." Sloane lays her hands in mine, her eyes on our union there. "But you're here," she says, her voice small and quiet.

I lift one hand to cup her chin and pull her eyes to me. "Yes," I tell her. "I am here. I am yours."

There is still a heavy look of disbelief in her eyes, and I feel the same—that we could be so lucky, that this could be true.

But she gasps once, a sob breaking through, and then she's in my arms, clinging to my neck, shuddering against me. I am too aware of Nazar and Devyn in the room with us still, otherwise I would soothe Sloane's fears deliberately so her body could shudder in more pleasurable ways.

But soon.

We have time now.

We have time, and no war to worry over, and no secrets to keep.

"Sloane," I say her name into her hair and pull back to kiss her.

The kiss is a promise.

It is a beginning.

EPILOGUE: SLOANE

"As the archmage's curse fades from Isaura's veins, she turns at last to her love, for the first time able to look on him with only a singular emotion driving her to action. She welcomes that emotion, dives headfirst into it, and with a cry of victory, Kilian claims his Dawn Queen in a kiss that remakes their world."

I shut the book and hold, waiting for a reaction.

Behind me, nestled in the blankets of our bed, Kilian's laughter rumbles through my chest. "That is a...colorful end."

I bark laughter and spin to face him. "Colorful? That's all you have to say?"

"What would you have me say?"

"I...I don't know! I feel like you should have some profound insight given that you're one of the titular characters."

"Ah. But am I?" His smile is teasing.

I roll my eyes. "Fine. We'll just call it *colorful.*" I toss *Fort of Night and Edge* to the foot of the bed. "Do you want to start number three? Ambrose comes back. You punch him in the face."

Kilian laughs again. Fuck, I will never get tired of that sound.

"As tempting as that may be to read about," he reaches for me and rolls me over him until I'm laying across his chest, "I do not think I need to hear more about this other Kilian. His actions are not mine, and his ending is not mine either."

I grin down at him and push forward to kiss him, light and quick, but I leave my lips over his. "No. It certainly is not."

With ever-perfect timing, my phone chirps.

It could be Eden. We're supposed to have a couple's date with her and her boyfriend tonight.

But more likely it's Devyn—since this whole *jumping timelines shifting reality one in a million chance* thing, I've taken on a sort of job at Club Reverie. Kilian, too. Letting her take various readings and going over in detail what we experienced in his world. She gets data, we get a job—and answers, maybe, about how this happened at all.

Though I couldn't give a fuck about answers.

I have everything I need.

I ignore the text alert. Whatever it is, it can wait.

"The one thing I did enjoy about those books," Kilian starts, his hands gripping my upper arms, "was a few of the lines. What was that one…ah."

He flips me, heaving me bodily so I'm the

one lying on the bed, his weight pressing down on me. I squeal, giddy and vibrant.

"'You will have me,'" Kilian quotes from the book. "'But only once you are dripping for me, my love. Only once your body is unwound will I push us both to that last glorious edge.'"

"Mm." I nip at his nose. "Glorious edge, huh?"

He nuzzles my neck, teeth grazing the skin as his hand works down to my belt. He doesn't undo it; his fingers slip right past the waistband and easily, effortlessly, hook up into my cunt.

I hiss, arching against his body, and he purrs his enjoyment.

"Oh, it will be glorious," he says into my neck. "To hear your moans. To feel your shudders. To taste your pleasure. How long will it take you to reach that edge, I wonder? Ten seconds, if memory serves."

I laugh, and he takes advantage of that distraction to press his thumb into my clit. He knows damn well that I could come right now if he told me to, but I bite my lips together, refusing to give him the satisfaction of a response.

He rubs my clit, a tight, quick circle, and when I don't so much as quiver, his purr turns to a growl.

"Sloane." He pulls up to stare down at me, his gaze heavy with intent and command. I squirm, shrieking with pleasure as he pumps his fingers into me, and his satisfied grin descends over me in a wave.

I near that glorious edge, and with his arms around me, I jump.

THE END

Stay up-to-date on releases from Natasha Luxe by joining her shared newsletter with Liza Penn!

You'll get double the spicy reads for one easy sign up. (But don't worry, we won't spam you—max two emails a month!)

https://rarebooks.substack.com/welcome

Read on for an exclusive excerpt from the next book in the Club Reverie series:

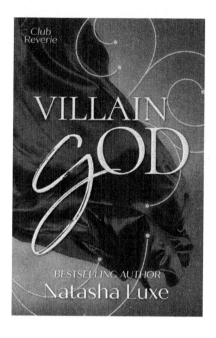

The origins of Club Reverie, where your dreams become your reality...

Devyn has combined her two obsessions: the first, a wildly popular sci-fi series about defying the limitations of time and space; and the second, an equally defying project that bends the lines between virtual and reality. She's managed to create a perfect virtual replica of her favorite sci-fi world, one that looks and feels entirely real—even populated by the enticing, dangerous characters she loves.

But just before she's due to present her creation to seek funding, one last trip inside puts her face to face with the world's deadliest villain: the immortal god, Nazar.

Devyn should be able to pull herself out with one button push…but Nazar's powers prevent her from leaving. Trapped as a prisoner of the man who has haunted her fantasies for years, she knows it isn't real—but that doesn't stop her from being drawn to the enticing, charismatic Nazar.

Devyn has spent her whole life studying the boundaries between fantasy and reality…but for Nazar, she might just break those boundaries entirely.

I see the product of the women's dressing-up now. My hair is twisted and braided in soft curls that hang around my face. My stomach is bare, chest teasingly covered by braided red fabric that connects to draping chains of gold around my shoulders. The skirt is sheer red and flows from my hips to the tops of my bare feet, showing my bare legs beneath, and when I shift against Nazar, I feel my complete lack of panties, the cool air kissing my damp pussy.

I'm a prize. A gift wrapped and ready to be opened.

Nazar's hand plants on my bare stomach and I instinctively arch into him. Something pokes my back—

Holy shit. That's his cock. His rock-hard cock, to be exact, and I go perfectly still, so aware of the way every breath makes my chest rise like an invitation.

Nazar meets my eyes in the mirror. "You are the prize. They will tear themselves to pieces over you."

One hand still splayed on my stomach, he lifts his other to wrap around my neck.

"But you can stop it all," he bends down to brush his nose against my ear, "by telling me why you are here."

I could just tell him. He wouldn't understand, but it'd be *something*, and maybe I could stop all of this.

But I don't want to.

I look fucking amazing, and I feel powerful because of it. My body aches with the sensations, the sweetness of Nazar's touch and the tension that permeates from his breath on my skin, and I realize how very long it's been since I felt *good* like this.

I'm stuck here for the time being.

So you know what?

I'm going to fucking enjoy myself.

"I'll tell you why I'm here," I whisper back to him.

I push my breasts out and grab his hand on my stomach.

Knotted together, our hands go down, down, to dip beneath the waistband of my skirt.

A low, heady growl starts in Nazar's chest. I can feel its vibrations wash in pinpricks of energy over my breasts as I maneuver his fingers to slide up into my cunt.

His fingers arch obediently and pump once, matching the strangled snarl that he buries in the side of my head, his breath so hot it nearly scalds me. I can't help the moan that grinds through my lips.

"But we're going to have some fun first," I add and quickly peel out of his arms.

Nazar stands there, hands out for one breath, before he cuts a glare to me so alive that I think, for a second, that I really fucked up.

His cock bulges against his tunic, but he ignores it to lift his fingers to his mouth and suck my juices off them.

All the while, glaring at me.

Holy shit.

One false move, and I have no doubt he'd heave me onto the bed and claim me as his own prize, threat be damned.

I could push it.

I could fuck Nazar.

But there's a flash of possession in his eyes, behind that glare. I wonder—will fucking a gladiator make him jealous?

Oh, that I have to see.

I shrug carelessly and give a cocky smirk.

Nazar's glare flinches. "Tell me your name."

I suck the inside of my cheek. But I relent. "Devyn."

"Devyn," he echoes, and I can feel each letter curl off his tongue. His wicked, wild tongue.

He stalks a step closer to me.

"Devyn," he says again. His voice is grating and rough, unsatisfied, untamed. He bends close to me. "You will regret tempting the god of discord."

Printed in Great Britain
by Amazon

80623987R00092